## THE FIRST WAVE

There was the sound of metal on metal as weapons were readied. Then, from a cloud of dust, the Comanches were there, arrows flying.

"Fire!" Ethan shouted.

The first volley of shots took Comanches from their horses, but that didn't stop the others from coming. Ethan and his men worked the levers on their rifles as quickly as they could. As the attacking Indians got closer, some of the men, who were more comfortable with them, pulled their pistols and brought them into play.

And just when Ethan thought the Comanches would keep coming and overrun them, they turned and headed back the way they had come. Some were injured and on foot, others lying face up or face down, dead.

It was over.

"That was the first wave!" Granger called out. "Get reloaded."

# RALPH COMPTON

# THE SAGEBRUSH TRAIL

A RALPH COMPTON WESTERN BY
# ROBERT J. RANDISI

BERKLEY
New York

BERKLEY

An imprint of Penguin Random House LLC

penguinrandomhouse.com

ISBN: 9780593334034

First Edition: November 2021

Printed in the United States of America
1   3   5   7   9   10   8   6   4   2

Book design by George Towne

# THE IMMORTAL COWBOY

This is respectfully dedicated to the "American Cowboy." His was the saga sparked by the turmoil that followed the Civil War, and the passing of more than a century has by no means diminished the flame.

———◆———

True, the old days and the old ways are but treasured memories, and the old trails have grown dim with the ravages of time, but the spirit of the cowboy lives on.

———◆———

In my travels—to Texas, Oklahoma, Kansas, Nebraska, Colorado, Wyoming, New Mexico, and Arizona—I always find something that reminds me of the Old West. While I am walking these plains and mountains for the first time, there is this feeling that a part of me is eternal, that I have known these old trails before. I believe it is the undying spirit of the frontier calling me, through the mind's eye, to step back into time. What is the appeal of the Old West of the American frontier?

———◆———

It has been epitomized by some as the dark and bloody period in American history. Its heroes—Crockett, Bowie, Hickok, Earp—have been reviled and criticized. Yet the Old West lives on, larger than life.

———◆———

It has become a symbol of freedom, when there was always another mountain to climb and another river to cross; when a dispute between two men was settled not with expensive lawyers, but with fists, knives, or guns. Barbaric? Maybe. But some things never change. When the cowboy rode into the pages of American history, he left behind a legacy that lives within the hearts of us all.

—*Ralph Compton*

# CHAPTER ONE

WHEN ETHAN MILLER bought his ranch it was called the Bar W. The first thing he did was change the name to Paradise. It had long been his ambition to have a large ranch. That's why he had been saving his pay from the army for many years. When he finally left the service, just after the war, he was able to buy the Bar W and rename it.

The ranch was located about ten miles outside of Bozeman, Montana. Ethan sat on his porch with a cup of coffee, watching the horses in the corral move about. This was just part of the herd he had amassed, which he was preparing to sell. He hoped that the proceeds from the sale would be what he had always imagined they would be.

He also watched his men as they did their work, preparing the horses to be driven to market. He just wasn't yet sure where they were going to drive them to.

Moses, his houseman, came out of the house with a pot of coffee.

"More coffee, suh?"

"Yes, Moze," Ethan said, "and how many times have I told you to stop calling me sir? We're not in the army anymore."

"Yes, Cap'n," the Black man said.

Moze stood there a moment, also staring at the corral.

"This looks jus' like you described all those times on the field, sir."

"Yes, Moze," Ethan said, "it does, doesn't it . . ."


## Virginia
## April 9, 1865

Captain Ethan Miller was serving in the Cavalry Corps of the army of the Potomac under General Philip Sheridan. He was sitting in his command tent, studying the map on the table before him, waiting to hear if they were going to go into battle in the morning.

Private Moses Jefferson came into the tent carrying a steaming plate of food and a cup of coffee.

"Supper, suh."

"Thanks, Moze," Ethan said. "Put it there." There was some space on the table that was not taken up by the map.

"Also," Moze said, "Lieutenant Ashforth wants ta see ya, suh."

Ethan sat back in his chair, grabbed his plate and fork and said, "Send 'im in, Moze."

"Yessuh."

Moze left and, moments later, a tall, slender man, fifteen years younger than Ethan, entered.

"I'll say it again, Captain," he said. "That nigger don't belong in this man's army. He's a goddamned slave."

"He was a slave, Lieutenant," Ethan said. "Then he became a free man and joined our side."

"To fight slavery," Ashforth said, shaking his head.

"Isn't that what we're all fightin'?" Ethan asked. He put some stew into his mouth.

"No," Ashforth said, "it ain't as simple as that, and you know it."

"Then what are you fightin' for, Lieutenant?" Ethan asked, pointing at the man with his fork.

"I'm fightin' for there to be one president," Lieutenant Ashforth said. "The one true president, Abraham Lincoln."

"What did you want, Lieutenant?" Ethan asked, putting the plate down.

"I think it's time to deploy the men, sir," Ashforth said.

"Not yet," Ethan said. "We're still waitin' to hear from Appomattox."

Ashforth snorted.

"You really think Lee's gonna surrender?"

"I'm hopin' he will," Ethan said. "Then I don't have to send these men into battle again."

"That's what they're here for," Ashforth said. "That's what *we're* here for. You may not like this war, but—"

"And you do?" Ethan asked, cutting the man off. "You like war, Lieutenant?"

"I'm not afraid of it," the younger man said. "If you want me to give the order, I will."

"Stand down, Lieutenant," Ethan said. "I'll let you know when I'm ready to give any orders."

Ashforth started to leave the tent, then stopped.

"You know, the men don't like you havin' that slave here."

"I told you, he's not a slave," Ethan said. "He's a soldier."

"Well, you treat him like a slave," Ashforth said. "He cooks for you, washes your uniform, shines your buttons—"

"I don't ask him to do any of those things," Ethan said. "He volunteers."

"Then maybe he likes bein' a slave," Ashforth said. "Maybe he should go back."

"He's bein' paid, Lieutenant," Ethan said, "just like the rest of us. Slaves were never paid. Go have your supper." Ethan picked his plate up again.

"Yes, sir."

Ashforth left the tent. Ethan took another bite of the stew, then set it down. He'd had enough of this war. If Lee didn't surrender, and he had to send his men into battle again in the morning . . .

He looked up as the tent flap was flipped again and another man walked in. He had sergeant's stripes on his arm. The only reason for that was that he would not accept a battlefield commission to lieutenant. He didn't want to be an officer.

"What'd he want?" Sergeant William Granger asked. At fifty he was only a year or two older than Ethan.

"War," Ethan said, "what else?"

"Too bad you have to have him as your second," Granger said.

"I wanted you as my second, but you won't take the promotion."

Granger made a face.

"I hate officers," he said. "I don't wanna be one."

"How are the men, Grange?" Ethan asked.

"Antsy," Granger said. "They want it to be over."

"So do I," Ethan said.

"Montana's callin' you?" Granger asked.

"You know it," Ethan said. "You're comin' with me, right?"

He'd asked the man half a dozen times already.

"I'll tell you what," Granger said, "I'll go with you, but I don't wanna be no foreman. I just wanna be a ranch hand."

"I need a foreman, Grange."

"You're gonna take some of the other men with you, right?" Granger asked.

"If they'll come," Ethan said.

"Make Taggart your foreman," Granger said. "He'll go with you, and he's a good man."

Corporal George Taggart *was* a good man, but he wasn't Granger.

"We'll see," Ethan said.

Granger pointed to the plate.

"Eat that," he said. "Who knows when we'll get hot food, again."

"You don't think Lee's gonna surrender, do you?" Ethan asked.

"No, I don't," Granger said, and left the tent.

Ethan picked up the plate and continued eating.

M OZE CAME IN later to collect the plate and hand Ethan a fresh cup of coffee.

"Thanks, Moze."

"Yessuh."

Before Moze could leave, Ethan said, "Tell me, Moze, what do you want to do after the war?"

"What can I do?" the Black man asked, with a shrug. Moze was supposed to be in his forties, but Ethan had the feeling he lied about his age to get into the Union Army. He suspected the man was in his sixties. "I been a slave my whole life."

"You're a free man now," Ethan said. "You can do whatever you want."

"Oh," Moze said, "I think we both knows that ain't true, Cap'n."

"Well then, how about you come along with me to my ranch in Montana?" Ethan said. "You can work for me. I'll pay you real well."

Moze smiled widely.

"I thought you'd never ask, Cap'n," he said. "I'll keep your house for you real good."

"We'll see what you're gonna do when we get there," Ethan said. "That's all."

"Yes, suh."

Moze started to leave, poking his head out, but then drew back in.

"They's a dispatch rider here with a message from headquarters, Cap'n."

Ethan stood.

"I guess that's what we've been waitin' for, Moze," he said. "Send 'im in."

Moze waved and stepped aside to let a man wearing corporal stripes to enter the tent.

"Captain Miller?" he asked.

"That's right."

"Dispatch, sir," the breathless corporal said, holding it out.

"Thank you, Corporal."

"You, uh, mind if I stay while you read it, sir?" the soldier asked.

"Why not?" Ethan asked. "You stayin', Moze?"

"Yessuh!" Moze looked outside. "And they's plenny others out here waitin', too."

"Well then," Ethan said, "let's not keep any of them waitin' any longer."

He opened the dispatch, read it, then looked at Moze and the corporal.

"Let's step outside," he said.

"Yessir," the corporal replied.

He and Moze left the tent, and Ethan followed.

Outside, standing in a semicircle, was a crowd of men, among them Lieutenant Ashforth.

"Men," Captain Ethan Miller said, "at one o'clock this afternoon, in the Appomattox Court House, General Robert E. Lee surrendered to General Ulysses S. Grant. It took a while for this word to reach us, but for all intents and purposes . . . the war is over! Or, as General Grant announced, the Rebels are our countrymen again."

The men began shouting and tossing their hats in the air, with the sole exception of Lieutenant Anthony Ashforth, who was scowling. Later he would be heard to say, "No Johnny Reb will ever be my countryman."

Ashforth, leading a band of men loyal to him, would go on fighting his war for a long time . . .

# CHAPTER TWO

*Bozeman, Montana*
*1867*

IN ADDITION TO Taggart and Granger, twelve of the men who served under Captain Ethan Miller came to Paradise with him. George Taggart agreed to be foreman. Moze came and accepted the job of taking care of Ethan and the house. It may have been similar to what he did as a slave, but he was being paid. His cousin Abraham, a freed slave, came later to cook for the men.

Bill Granger, who had been friends with Ethan before they went into the army, agreed to work for him, but reinforced that he wanted to be only a hand, not a foreman.

"Supper be ready in ten minutes," Moze announced. "Is Mr. Granger comin' tonight?"

"Yeah, he'll be here."

Most of the time Ethan ate in his house alone. He

enjoyed the serenity. He was used to eating with the sound of artillery in the distance. However, in the mornings he went to the mess hall and had breakfast with the men. He felt it was important to keep in contact with them, and let them know he was no longer "Captain" Miller, even though he was their superior.

While Moze cooked supper for him every night, Abraham cooked for the men. When they went on a drive, Moze rode in the chuck wagon with his cousin, and they shared the duties.

Everything Ethan had wanted for Paradise had pretty much come to fruition. The only problem he still had was income. The horses he had now—half of them wild, half animals that he had bred—were supposed to bring in a good chunk of money. They represented security and could set him up for the life he wanted. If it happened, he would be amazed that it had taken only two years.

He was getting ready to go inside for supper when he saw Granger approaching the house.

"Hungry?" Ethan asked.

"Starvin'," Granger said.

"Moze says supper's on the table," Ethan said, standing and tossing away the stub of his cigar.

"Let's go!" Granger said.

In the beginning Granger had felt uncomfortable eating in the house with Ethan. Not because they were friends, but because it made him stand out from the other men. That was why he told Ethan that he would eat with him "occasionally" and not every night. He felt it was more important that he eat with the other hands.

Taggart, as foreman, also made sure to eat with the men. On rare occasions, Ethan would invite him to his table, but it was usually so they could discuss business.

Over a supper of fried chicken, vegetables, and biscuits, Ethan asked, "How's everythin' goin'?"

"Most of the horses are ready to go," Granger said. "There are still some wild ones up in the Big Sky Meadow that we have to round up, but we can get that done tomorrow."

"That's good."

"What about the buyer?" Granger asked.

"I'm goin' to Bozeman tomorrow," Ethan said. "There should be a telegram waitin' for me."

"You think you're gonna get your price?"

"I hope so."

"A hundred and fifty a head?" Granger said. "In the war we could get a horse for ten dollars."

"'Ten-dollar horse, forty-dollar saddle,' right?" Ethan quoted.

"I remember that," Granger said, with a smile.

"If I get that price everybody gets a bonus, and we stay afloat for a long time to come," Ethan said.

"And who's this buyer, again?"

"Some sort of international circus that needs horses," Ethan said.

"Wow," Granger said. "So these horses would be goin' toward entertainin' people, not killin' 'em."

"That's the idea." Ethan grabbed another chicken breast. Moze knew he liked them, so when he cooked chicken it was mostly breasts. "How are the men?"

"They're all set," Granger said. "Taggart's assigned them their jobs and they're ready."

"So I guess the rest is up to me," Ethan said.

Granger poked around in the pile of chicken on the platter in the center of the table.

"No legs?"

"All breasts, remember?" Ethan said. "You want legs, tell Abraham."

"Right." He grabbed a breast, took a big bite. "Takin' anybody to town with you tomorrow?"

"I wasn't going to," Ethan said. "You wanna come?"

"Yeah, I do."

"Fine. Meet me out front at nine, after breakfast."

Granger nodded.

After supper they sat on the porch together, smoked cigars, and drank coffee.

"It's been two years, you know," Ethan said. "You can move into the house. I'll even give you a piece of Paradise."

"This place is yours," Granger said, "your dream. I just wanna work the horses."

"Okay," Ethan said, with a smile, "so take your cigar and get off my porch. I'll see you in the mornin'."

Granger laughed and left the porch.


IN THE MORNING Ethan went to the mess and had flapjacks and bacon with Granger, Taggart, and the men.

"Grange says you're goin' to Bozeman today," Taggart said.

"That's right."

"Makin' your sale?"

"Yep."

Taggart stacked the flapjacks high on his plate.

"I'll have the men ready by the time you get back."

"You'll have those horses from the meadow?"

"Oh, yeah," Taggart said. "I'm goin' out there myself with three men."

"Good. I want to be ready to leave as soon as we get the word."

"We'll be ready, boss," Taggart said.

Granger was sitting at the other end of the long table. When breakfast was over and all the men started to leave the mess, Ethan walked over to the house and found Granger already waiting there with their horses.

"I didn't ask you to saddle my horse," he said.

"Hey," Granger said, "you're the boss, remember?" They mounted up and headed for Bozeman.

Bozeman had been founded only three years earlier by John Bozeman, who also established the Bozeman Trail, which led to Virginia City.

For a town only three years old, however, it was growing in leaps and bounds, especially since gold had been discovered near Virginia City. But all Ethan felt he needed from it was the mercantile and the telegraph office. His men made use of the saloon, whorehouses, and cafés, all of which he had visited very rarely—or in the case of the whorehouse, not at all.

When they rode in Granger said, "I'll hit the mercantile."

"I just need to stop at the telegraph office," Ethan said.

"Meet at the Yellowstone Saloon for a beer?"

"It's a little early," Ethan said, "but if you insist."

"Just one before we head back," Granger said.

"Okay, Grange," Ethan said. "See you there."

They split up, Granger riding to the mercantile while Ethan reined in his horse in front of the stage line office. They had a telegraph key there that they allowed him to use.

"Mornin', Cap'n," the clerk said, as he entered. He used the office enough for the man to recognize him.

"Mornin', Bob," he said, remembering the man's name. "Anythin' for me?"

"Yeah, you got one," Bob said. "Came in yesterday. Here ya go."

Ethan stepped outside the office before he opened the telegram and read it.

* * *

WHEN GRANGER ENTERED the saloon he saw that Ethan not only had a beer in front of him at the bar, but a glass of whiskey. As he approached he waved at the bartender for the same thing. This early the saloon was almost empty, so the two men had the bar—and the bartender—to themselves.

Granger drank down his shot of whiskey and stared at his friend.

"Bad news?"

"You know," Ethan said, "I fought off the Crow and the Sioux to get Paradise up and running, and now I'm gonna get shut down by some goddamned circus."

"They ain't makin' the buy?" Granger asked.

Ethan handed Granger the telegram as his answer, and waved at the bartender for another whiskey.

"'Plans have changed'?" Granger said. "That's their explanation?"

"Sons of bitches!" Ethan growled.

Granger laid the telegram down on the bar. Not only did his friend not get his price, he wasn't getting the sale, at all.

"Well," he said, "you didn't let the Crow or Sioux stop you, and you won't let this stop you, either."

Ethan held the shot of whiskey halfway to his mouth and lowered it.

"No," he said. "No I won't."

Granger took the shot of whiskey from Ethan's hand and drank it down.

"So drink your beer and go send some more telegrams," he told Ethan. "I'll wait right here."

"Here?" Ethan said.

"Well, one of us has to get drunk, and one has to stay sober," Granger said. "Which do you wanna do?"

"I know which one I wanna do," Ethan said, "but that ain't what I'm gonna do."

"I figured."

"But first I gotta think," Ethan said.

"You got a whole beer to do your thinkin' over," Granger told him.

With that they both leaned over their beers on the bar and fell silent.

A FEW MEN CAME and went during Ethan's think, but he finally made his way to the bottom of his beer mug and pushed it away.

"You got it?" Granger asked.

"I got it," Ethan said. "I hope."

"Whataya gonna do?"

"I'll send a few telegrams," Ethan said, "but it ain't gonna happen today."

"As long as you get somethin' goin'," Granger said. "We still got time to get the herd together."

Ethan straightened. "You still gonna stay here, or will I have to come and drag you out of the whorehouse?"

"Let's see," Granger said, "beer, or whore."

"You make up your mind," Ethan said. "If I don't find you here, I'll know where to look."

Ethan turned and left the saloon.

"Wow," the bartender said, "I thought when he came in here that he was gonna tie one on. You sure talked him out of it."

"I just had to get 'im so he talked himself out of it," Granger said. "Hit me again, Zeke."

# CHAPTER THREE

Ethan was only two years removed from having been a captain in the Union Army. Hopefully, he still had a few connections in the government. He sent telegrams to the three people he thought would be of assistance, including General Phil Sheridan. Once they were sent he told the clerk he'd be at the Yellowstone Saloon, waiting for replies.

If he still had the connections he thought he had, the replies would come in that day. If not, he might have to go back to the Paradise and wait there for a few days.

When he got back to the Yellowstone, Granger was still standing at the bar. There were a few more customers than when he left, but not many. Others were just starting to trickle in.

"What's the verdict?" Granger asked him.

"The jury's still out," Ethan said. "Hopefully, I'll get some replies today, including one that I particularly want."

"Then I guess you want another beer."

"Sure, why not?"

"And whiskey?"

"No," Ethan said, "I've had enough."

The bartender, Zeke, set two more beers up for them.

"Let's sit," Ethan said.

They had their choice of empty tables, and simply took the nearest one.

"So, the army?" Granger asked.

"Yeah," Ethan said, glumly.

"I thought you didn't want your horses goin' to war?" Granger said.

"It doesn't look like I have that option," Ethan said.

"Where are we gonna have to drive them to?"

"I'm hoping Fort Ellis."

Fort Ellis wasn't far. It had been set up to protect settlers and gold miners from the Indians, who were not happy about what the whites were doing to their land.

"Did you send a telegram to Sheridan?"

"I did."

"See, that had to hurt you."

"This whole situation is hurtin' me, Grange," Ethan said, "but what can I do? I have two hundred horses that have to be sold and a dozen men who have to be paid."

"You know," Granger said, "the military never understood why you didn't want to stay and accept those major bars."

"I know."

"They might try to use this to get you back in."

"We'll see," Ethan said. "If they're still upset that I didn't accept the promotion, we may not hear from them at all."

"I guess," Granger said, "we ought to plan on eating supper in town, tonight."

Ethan nodded, absently. "And you know just the place, don't you?" he asked.

"Well, I've eaten in a few places, but the one I could never get into was the Cattleman's Club. But you could get us in."

"I'm not a cattleman," Ethan pointed out.

"They serve anybody who owns a ranch," Granger said.

"Ah."

"So?"

"So why not?" Ethan said. "Might as well have a good meal while we wait."

"It's too early now," Granger pointed out. "What do we do in the meantime?"

"In the meantime," Ethan said, "we just wait."

B Y THE TIME suppertime came around no reply was forthcoming from the military.

"We might as well go and eat," Ethan said.

They stopped at the bar and told the bartender where they'd be in case the telegraph key operator came looking.

"You think they're gonna let you in?" he asked. "You ain't cattlemen."

"We'll see," Ethan said.

They left the saloon and headed for the Club.

E THAN HAD NEVER been there before, so he left it up to Granger to find the place. When they reached the two-story structure there was a large man barring the way. He stood in front of the door with his hands behind his back.

"Can't go in," he told them, as they climbed the stairs.

"Why not?" Ethan asked.

"You ain't members."

"How do you know that?"

The man grinned, revealing several spaces in his smile where teeth used to reside.

"I know all the members," he said. "You been invited by a member?"

"No," Ethan said, "but—"

"Do you know who this man is?" Granger asked.

"No, I don't," the man admitted. "But I've heard that line before."

"This is Captain Ethan Miller," Granger said, "owner of the Paradise Ranch."

"The Paradise," the man repeated. "That's a pretty big place."

"Yes, it is," Ethan said.

"Captain?" the man said.

"Retired," Ethan said.

"Which side?"

"North."

"You got cattle on the Paradise?"

Ethan shook his head.

"I raise horses," he said. "Right now I've got two hundred sitting out there, ready to be drove to market."

"Well," the man said, "I guess we could make an exception. That is, if you really are who you say you are."

"How would you like me to prove it?" Ethan asked.

"Well—"

"I'm sure there's gonna be somebody inside who'll recognize him," Granger said. "If there ain't, you can toss us out, then."

The man gave that some thought, then said, "That's fair." He opened the door. "Go on in, gents."

"Thank you," Ethan said.

He and Granger entered. Immediately they smelled

leather, cigar smoke, and steak. They followed their noses to a dining room that seemed to be half-filled.

A man in his thirties—with a self-important expression—approached them and said, "I'm sorry, sirs, but it's members only."

Before Ethan could speak someone across the room called out, "Hold it there, Edward."

Edward, Ethan, and Granger all turned toward the voice, saw a large man approaching, with a prodigious belly and broad smile preceding him. He was in his fifties, gray-haired, and stretching the seams of his suit.

When he reached them he said to Edward, "Don't you know who this is?"

"Uh, no, sir, I don't," the tall, slender Edward said.

"This here's Captain Ethan Miller, late of the Union Army," the man said. "He also happens to own the Paradise spread."

"That may be, Mr. Proctor, but he's still not a member—"

"Well, I am, and these boys are my guests," Proctor said. "So just go off and do your job somewhere else. Go on, git!"

Edward almost seemed hurt as he slunk off.

"You're Oswald Proctor," Ethan said. "You own the biggest cattle spread in the county."

"That's right, I do," Proctor said. "Why don't you two gents come on over and sit at my table."

"Much obliged, Mr. Proctor," Ethan said.

"Oh, hell, we're gonna have supper together," Proctor said. "Just call me Oswald."

Before Ethan or Granger could say anything else the man headed back to his table. When they got there, they saw that it was set up for four, with all four chairs already taken.

"You boys go and sit at another table," Proctor said to two of them.

The two middle-aged men he had spoken to looked shocked and said, "But Mr. Proctor, we're doing business—"

"We're finished with our business, Borden," Proctor said. "The answer's no. Now, you're still my guests here, but I want you to go and eat at another table. Pronto!"

The two men got to their feet and stumbled off in a daze.

"Have a seat, gents," Proctor said to Ethan and Granger. "This here's my foreman, Ed Tobin."

Tobin, a cowhand in his late forties, nodded to both of them.

"Ed, this here's Captain Ethan Miller, and . . . I didn't get your name, son."

"This is Bill Granger," Ethan introduced his companion.

"Foreman?" Proctor asked, as he sat.

"Friend," Ethan said.

"I also work on the ranch," Granger said.

When they were all seated Proctor said, "We were just about to order supper. You mind if I do it for all of us?"

"Not at all," Ethan said.

Proctor called the waiter over and ordered four steak dinners.

"And boy," he said, to the young waiter, "I want the four biggest steaks you got in that kitchen."

"Yessir."

"And four beers."

"Yessir."

The waiter hurried off.

"Some of these fellas put on airs and order wine with their steaks," Oswald said. "Not me. I'm a plain man, Captain."

"You can call me Ethan, Oswald."

"You fought in the war," Proctor said. "You deserve to be called Captain." He looked at Granger. "Were you in the war?"

"I was," Granger said, "right at the Captain's side. I was a sergeant."

"I wanted to give him a battlefield promotion more times than I can count," Ethan said. "He refused every time."

"I'm a plain man, too, Oswald."

"Well, I sure as hell respect that!" Proctor said. "What brings you to the Cattleman's Club?"

"Seriously," Ethan said. "I was doin' some business in town, and I'm waitin' on some telegrams. We got hungry, but I don't come to town much. I didn't know where to go and eat until Grange commented on how good the food is supposed to be here. And he said we'd be welcome because I own a ranch, even if it's not a cattle ranch."

"Well, he was wrong there," Proctor said. "Fact is, if I wasn't here and happened to recognize you, you wouldn't be sittin' here waitin' on a steak."

"How did you recognize me?" Ethan asked.

"Oh, it was a while back, when you first came to town," Proctor said. "I saw you comin' out of the bank, and I asked. I'm nosy, that way."

"That was two years ago," Ethan said.

"I have a good memory," Proctor said.

The waiter came and set four beers down on the table.

"Steaks are comin' right out, Mr. Proctor."

"Good boy!" Proctor said.

"They treat you good here," Granger said.

"This place wouldn't even be here without Mr. Proctor," the foreman said.

"I'm just an investor," Proctor said.

"Your money built this whole place," Tobin said.

"Ed's real loyal to me," Proctor said. He picked up his beer mug. "Here's to new friends."

Granger picked his glass up. Ethan hesitated, then did the same.

"New friends," he said.

# CHAPTER FOUR

I N THE MIDDLE of their meal, while Proctor was talk-ing about his upbringing, the man from out front appeared in the doorway. Edward went to see what he wanted, and the doorman handed him something. Edward turned and walked to Proctor's table.

". . . wouldn't think a twenty-year-old could make that work, but I did it—" Proctor stopped short and looked at Edward. "What is it?"

"Telegram for your guest, sir."

"Well, give it to 'im."

Edward handed Ethan the telegram.

"Thank you."

"Yes, sir." Edward walked away, shoulders stiff, still miffed.

Ethan put the telegram in his pocket.

"Ain't you gonna read it?" Proctor asked.

"Later," Ethan said. "You're tellin' a story and I don't want to be rude."

"Wow," Proctor said, "I sure admire that. I get one of those things, I've gotta read it right away."

"Whether I read it now or later ain't gonna change what it says," Ethan said. "I'd rather finish this great meal."

"I can understand that," Proctor said.

Ethan exchanged a glance with Granger before he said, "Why don't you continue with your story."

"Oh, of course," the rancher said. "Now, where was I . . ."


THEY FINISHED THEIR meal, topping it off with apple pie and coffee.

"Would you gents like to come to the smoking room and enjoy a cigar?"

"Why not?" Ethan said, and Granger nodded. "But don't we need to settle up—"

"Like I said," Proctor replied, cutting Ethan off, "you're my guests. Don't worry about the cost."

The four men stood and Ethan and Granger followed Proctor and his foreman to the smoking room. There were red leather chairs everywhere, surrounding a round table on which sat leather boxes Ethan assumed held the cigars.

As they sat in a grouping of chairs Proctor leaned over and opened a box.

"Help yourselves," he said. "You might want to light up and then read that telegram of yours while it's still early enough to do some business—if that's what you'll have to do."

Ethan didn't think it was still early enough to do business, but he was curious about what the telegram said, so he lit the cigar, sat back, and opened the message up.

He read it twice before refolding it and tucking it away.

"Ethan?" Granger asked.

Ethan hesitated.

"You can go ahead and discuss your business here," Proctor said. "That's what this place is for."

Ethan spoke to Granger.

"I was hoping the military would need horses for Fort Ellis or Fort Meagher," he said.

"So no takers?" Granger asked.

"They need horses at Fort Davis."

"Fort Davis?" Granger said. "In Texas?"

Ethan nodded.

"That's a long way to drive a herd," Proctor said.

"Yeah, it is," Ethan agreed.

"Are you at least gettin' your price?" the cattle rancher asked.

"We'll find out," Ethan said. "They're sending a representative here to negotiate."

"So we ain't startin' our drive in the next few days," Granger said.

"It doesn't look like it," Ethan said. "They're sending a Lieutenant Brodie here next week."

"Brodie," Granger said. "Don't know him."

"He's from the quartermaster's department, of course," Ethan said.

"If you don't mind me askin'," Proctor said, "why don't you find a private buyer rather than a military one?"

"I had a private buyer," Ethan said. "This trip to town was supposed to seal the deal, but instead I received an earlier telegram sayin' the deal was off."

"Ouch!" Proctor said.

"I know," Ethan said. "We were gettin' ready to leave tomorrow. Now we'll have to put the drive off at least a week."

"Losing a week can sometimes affect the condition of steer by the time we get them to market," Proctor said. "I imagine the same might be true for horses."

"It might," Ethan said. "That's why they're sending someone to inspect the horses before they commit." Ethan looked at Granger. "And we gotta make sure the horses look good when that lieutenant arrives."

"I know the Union Army had a preference for Morgans," Proctor said. "You ain't got no Morgans, do you?"

"Not a one," Ethan said. "I've got some good wild stock. I've managed to put together everything from buckskins to duns, roans, grulla, even some palominos."

"Any Pryor Mountain stock?"

"If they managed to drift over to my range, yeah," Ethan said, "but that's kind of far for us to go when we've got plenty of wild horses in Gallatin County. Anyway, the army's gonna have to take what they can get if they need 'em that bad."

*Unfortunately,* Ethan thought, *I might have to take what I can get, too.*

"I wish I could help you with a buyer," Proctor said, "but all my connections are in the cattle business."

"That's okay," Ethan said. "We appreciate the thought, and the meal, but I guess we better be goin'."

"You stop in here any time, Ethan," Proctor said. "You'll always be on the list as a guest of mine."

"Much obliged, Oswald," Ethan said, as they shook hands with the rancher and his foreman.

He and Granger took their leave.

OUTSIDE THEY WALKED down the steps of the Cattleman's Club and then stopped.

"Brodie," Granger said. "That name still ain't ringin' any bells."

"How many officers did you ever know from the quartermaster's department?" Ethan asked. "Besides, he's probably a young kid."

"You think they'd send a youngster to look at our horses?" Granger asked.

"Who knows what the army's gonna do," Ethan said.

"I think he'll be older," Granger said. "They're gonna wanna dicker with you, Ethan. They'll wanna get those horses as cheap as they can."

"It'll all depend on how bad they need 'em," Ethan said. "Come on, let's get back to the ranch."

"It's gettin' dark," Granger observed.

"We know the way," Ethan said.

WHEN THEY GOT back to the Paradise, Granger said he would take care of the horses.

"Come inside for a drink when you're finished," Ethan told him.

That told Granger that his friend needed to talk.

As Ethan entered the house, Moze approached and took his hat and gun.

"It didn't go well, suh?" Moze asked.

"Can you tell?" Ethan said.

"I can always read the look on yo face, suh."

"Then no, it didn't go well," Ethan said. "We have to wait for a visit next week from someone from the army quartermaster," Ethan explained.

Moze scowled and said, "The army, suh?"

"I know, I know," Ethan said. "I feel the same way. But he'll be our guest. We'll put him in one of the upstairs rooms."

"Yes, suh."

"Grange is comin' in for a drink," he told Moze. "He should be in any minute. Let him go into the sittin' room and get his drink."

"Yes, suh."

Ethan went into the room he had arranged as a sitting room and office. When he bought the ranch there was already a house on the land. Not exactly what he would have built. It was too large, had too many rooms, for a bachelor with no wife and family; so, he chose to remain on the first floor, leaving the second floor bedrooms for guests. He set up his sitting room-cum-office downstairs, and a room in the rear of the first floor as a bedroom. When he did have guests it was always for business, and this allowed them to have privacy on the second floor, and him the same on the first.

Ethan went to his bedroom to change clothes. When he got to the sitting room, Granger was already there, holding a healthy glass of whiskey and looking out the front window into the darkness.

"You know, if this was my house I woulda made this my bedroom."

"Well, let me give you part of the business," Ethan told him, "and you can move in and have your own bedroom anywhere you want."

Granger shook his head. "Too many headaches. I mean, look at what happened today."

Ethan walked to a small table where he kept some bottles and poured himself a whiskey. Then he looked at his desk, but walked over and sat in his favorite leather easy chair, settling in with a sigh.

"I thought I had this figured," he said.

"Ethan," Granger began, "you've managed to come a long way in two years. To me, you're a runaway train. You're not about to let some circus knock you off the tracks."

"The circus is out, the army is in," Ethan said. "We just have to convince this lieutenant from the quartermaster that the horses are worth what we're askin'."

"They are worth it," Granger said, turning from the

window. "You can't let some wet-behind-the-ears lieutenant tell you they ain't."

"This is gonna be interestin'," Ethan said. "I'm expectin' some kid, and you're waitin' for some grizzled veteran. If he's gonna be makin' this decision, he's gotta have some miles on 'im."

"West Point," Granger said, "he's gonna be some young idiot from West Point, mark my words."

"You wanna put your money where your mouth is?" Ethan asked.

"How much?" Granger said. "Just don't make it a month's pay."

"A week?"

"You got a bet," Granger said.

He drained his glass and went over and got Ethan's glass, filled both and brought Ethan's back to him so they could drink to it.

"This is good," Ethan said, "because if I don't get the deal, I'm gonna need the money."

# CHAPTER FIVE

THE NEXT MORNING Ethan staggered out of bed to have breakfast with the men and give them the news. Granger was also present, looking bleary-eyed.

"It looks like we're gonna have more time to get these horses ready to travel," Ethan announced, before Abraham brought the food out. "My original deal fell through, but the military is sending a man here next week to negotiate in good faith for the horses."

"The army," somebody said, with disgust.

"I know," Ethan said. "Most of us don't have fond feelin's for the army, but their money's gonna be the right color. So eat hearty, we got lots of work to do to make sure this herd is the best we can make it."

After breakfast Ethan took George Taggart aside.

"I'm sorry I didn't let you in on all of this first," he said. "I probably should've pulled you aside—"

"Don't worry about it, boss," Taggart said. "The army's not gonna find anythin' to complain about."

"Thanks, George."

As Taggart walked away, Granger came over.

"He okay?" he asked.

"He's fine," Ethan said. "I tried to apologize for not talkin' to him about all this first, but . . . he's fine with it."

"He's a good man," Granger said.

"That's why he's my foreman," Ethan said. "Well, that and the fact that you wouldn't take the job."

"I'm gonna go and see what the foreman wants me to do," Granger said, with a grin, and walked away.

While Taggart and Granger took the men out to the meadow, Ethan decided to spend the day at the corral, looking over the stock he had there. Taggart had the right attitude. They couldn't afford to have the army criticize any of the animals. To that end, Ethan spent the day cutting animals out of the herd that he thought might not pass muster with someone from the army quartermaster.

B Y THE END of the day he had cut a dozen horses from the corral. The question now was, what to do with them? He couldn't just let them to return to the wild, because then his men would probably end up bringing them back. So he moved them to a second corral, behind the barn. He'd take the matter up with Taggart and Granger.

When they came riding back in with the men, he intercepted them on the way to the bunkhouse.

"How'd it go?" he asked.

"The army should be impressed," Taggart said.

"Bein' out there today just reminded us of what good stock we've got," Granger said. "What's in the back corral?"

"Just some of the ones I weeded out," Ethan said.

"Ethan, you can't worry—" Granger started, but Ethan cut him off.

"I'd like you both to come and have supper at my house," he said. "Six o'clock, okay?"

"Fine with me," Taggart said.

"Me, too," Granger said.

"See ya then," Ethan said, and walked to the house. Granger and Taggart started for the bunkhouse.

"What d'ya think is on his mind?" Taggart asked.

"Business, I guess," Granger said.

"You know those horses in the front corral were fine, right?"

"I know," Granger said.

"We gotta keep him from havin' second thoughts about these animals, Grange," Taggart said. "This is good stock, both the wild and the ones we bred."

"I know, Taggart," Granger said. He called him Taggart because he knew his friend hated his first name. "Let's just hope we can convince him."

"I wanna take a look at those horses before we go to the house," Taggart said.

"We both will," Granger said, "but let's get cleaned up first."

"Okay."

There were a couple of barrels of water outside the bunkhouse that the hands used to clean up when they came in off the range. By the time they got there, they had to stand in line.

E THAN ENTERED THE house and shouted, "Moze!" Moze came running out from where he had been.

"Yeah, boss?"

"Two guests for supper," Ethan said. "Taggart and Granger."

"Right, boss," Moze said.

"Make something fillin'," Ethan instructed. "And some dessert."

"Pie, boss?"

"Cobbler, if Abraham can do it."

Moze smiled.

"Come on, boss," he said, "you knows he kin do anything."

"You're right, Moze," Ethan said. "I do know that. I'm gonna get cleaned up and changed."

"What time supper, boss?" Moze asked.

"Six."

"On the dot!" Moze said.

Ethan went to his bedroom as Moze went to the kitchen.

A T A QUARTER to six Granger and Taggart walked over to the back corral.

"You see anythin' wrong with these?" Taggart asked, as they leaned on the fence.

"No, I don't."

"This is money on the hoof," Taggart said. "We gotta keep him from wastin' it."

"He'll listen."

"What makes you say that?"

"Because it's both of us," Granger said.

"What d'ya think about sellin' to the army?" Taggart asked.

"I would've preferred sellin' to the circus," Granger said, "but what can we do? They dropped out."

"We could look for another circus," Taggart said, and then laughed.

"We *could* look for another buyer," Granger agreed, "but that would take a while, and these animals are in shape now. As it is they're gonna lose some weight on the drive."

"Do we know where we'll be drivin' them to?" Taggart asked.

"Ethan said something about Fort Davis."

"Texas!" Taggart gasped. "That's a thousand miles."

"More like fourteen hundred," Granger said.

"That's gonna take two months," Taggart said. "The army's gotta be able to get horses from somewhere closer."

Granger shrugged.

"Let's listen to what Ethan has to say," he said, "and then the officer from the quartermaster."

Taggart made a sour face.

"Officers!" he spat.

"Ethan was an officer," Granger reminded him.

"You know he was like no other officer we ever had," Taggart said. "That's the only reason we all followed him here."

"And he's made somethin' of this place," Granger said. "A home for all of us."

"Speakin' of home," Taggart said, "I'm ready for some home cookin'."

Granger laughed and said, "Don't let Abraham hear you say that. It'll give him a swelled head."

They left the corral and walked to the house.

E THAN ANSWERED THE knock at the door himself. "C'mon in," he told his two men. He considered both of them employees and friends. "Let's have a drink before supper."

He took them into the sitting room and gave each a shot of whiskey.

"Boss," Taggart said, "we stopped at the back corral on the way here. Those horses look fine."

"Do they?" Ethan asked.

"They do, Ethan," Granger said.

"You might be right," Ethan said.

"You can't let the army start you second-guessin'

your stock," Taggart told him. "That's how they'll drive the price down."

"I'll take another look at them tomorrow," Ethan said. "Maybe I overreacted."

Moze came to the door.

"Supper be ready," he said.

They left the sitting room and went to the dining room.

O VER SUCCULENT HUNKS of pork and expertly cooked vegetables, they talked some more about the stock, both in the corrals and out on the meadow. Over apple cobbler and coffee Ethan started asking the question he wanted to ask.

"Is there gonna be anybody in the bunkhouse who won't want to drive this herd to Fort Davis because they don't wanna work for the army?"

"Some of them might not like it," Taggart said, "but the men will follow you anywhere, boss. In war, and in peacetime. You know that."

Ethan looked at Granger.

"I can't think of anybody," he said. "I agree with Taggart."

"I'd like you both with me when I meet with this quartermaster," Ethan said. "I want your input."

"I think Taggart should be there because he's foreman," Granger said. "I ain't sure why you want me."

"Well, for one thing," Ethan said, "we have a bet."

"Oh, that."

"What bet?" Taggart asked.

"I think the army is gonna send us a wet-behind-the-ears West Pointer to deal with. Grange thinks it's gonna be a seasoned veteran."

"What if it ain't either?" Taggart asked.

"Then we both lose," Taggart said.

"Then who gets the money?"

Ethan and Granger looked at each other.

"I think somebody should hold the money, and if you both lose, they should keep it," Taggart suggested.

"And are you sayin' you should be that somebody?" Granger asked.

"Well, thank you, Grange," Taggart said. "I'd be happy to."

"You ain't gettin' any money unless you bet," Ethan said.

"Fine," Taggart said, "Grizzled old vet, wet-behind-the-ears . . . I say a mature, smart officer, not too young, not too old. That do ya?"

"That's fine," Granger said.

"What's the bet?" Taggart asked.

"A week's pay," Ethan said.

Taggart almost choked on the water he started to drink.

"Whose pay?" he demanded.

# CHAPTER SIX

T HEY SPENT THE weekend gathering the herd into the Big Sky Meadow, from where they would start the drive. The horses they kept in the corral were the ones they would show the army, to represent their stock.

On Monday Ethan got a telegram saying that Lieutenant Brodie would arrive on Wednesday's stage. Ethan told Taggart and Granger that they would all meet him.

"You gonna put 'im up here?" Granger asked.

"Sure," Ethan said. "I've got all those empty bedrooms upstairs."

"How's Moze feel about taking care of a military man?" Taggart asked.

"Moze'll do anythin' I ask him to do," Ethan said. "No matter how he feels about it."

"Do you expect us to eat with 'im?" Granger asked.

"I don't know," Ethan said. "I ain't decided that yet. Let's see what happens when he gets here."

The day the stage was to arrive they all went to town early, had breakfast in a small café, and then waited.

"Why don't we wait in the saloon?" Taggart asked.

"I don't want this lieutenant smellin' liquor on our breath."

"And what if he wants a drink after his long trip?" Granger asked.

"That'll be different," Ethan said. "We'll give 'im what he wants."

"So what do we do in the meantime?" Granger asked.

"We wait at the stage station," Ethan said. "The stage should be pullin' in soon."

The three of them walked to the station, which still had a new shine to it. They went inside, where there were wooden benches. Passengers waited there so they could board the stage after others left it.

"Afternoon, gents," the clerk said. "Gotta send a telegram?"

Ethan didn't use the telegraph office in town because he didn't want anyone knowing his business. He was pretty sure the clerk, Bob, kept Ethan's correspondence to himself. Bob was in the army for over twenty years, but mustered out before the war. They wouldn't take him back because of his age.

"No," Ethan said, "waitin' for the stage. Is it gonna to be on time?"

"Should be," Bob said. "I ain't heard otherwise."

"That's good."

"So yer all waitin' to greet . . . your guest?" Bob knew who was coming in because he was the one who got the telegrams.

"Yep," Taggart said, "we're all waitin'."

Bob looked at the clock on the wall, and then his pocket watch.

"Should be any minute," he said.

It turned out to be half an hour later when they

heard the stage rumbling up. The three of them got up, and Granger and Taggart followed Ethan out. Bob went to his ticket window to look out.

The station had a couple of men who handled the horses and got the luggage down from the top. They worked while the driver and shotgun dropped down, and the passengers started to disembark. Two men stepped out carrying the cases belonging to drummers, and then the third man out was a soldier.

"I win," Taggart said to the other two.

The lieutenant was neither young nor old. He was tall, fit, in his forties, looked like a man who had been in the service for some time, and would probably die in uniform, or retire at a ripe old age.

"Lieutenant Brodie?" Ethan asked, stepping forward.

"Captain Miller?" the man asked.

"Not anymore," Ethan said, as they shook hands. "This is Taggart, my foreman, and Granger, my top hand."

The lieutenant shook hands with all of them.

"Granger," he said, "you were a sergeant, right?"

"That's right."

"How'd you know that?" Ethan asked.

"Your unit was very effective durin' the war," Brodie said. "I made a point of familiarizing myself with you when I got this assignment." He looked at Granger again. "Seems to me you should've got a battlefield promotion at some point."

"I probably proposed it six times," Ethan said. "He refused each time."

"Didn't want to be an officer," Granger said.

"Can't say I blame you," Brodie said. "It's no picnic."

"We've got a buckboard over here for you and your bags," Ethan said.

"Just one bag," Brodie said. He looked up just as

one of the men tossed it down, and he caught it. "Ready to go."

"You'll be stayin' at the ranch," Ethan said. "That'll give you plenty of time to check the stock."

"I'm sure they'll be fine," Brodie said. "Sendin' me here was just a formality."

Ethan didn't believe that. The army wouldn't have sent an officer unless he was going to make some decisions while he was there.

They got Brodie up onto the buckboard, tossed his bag in the back, and Taggart took the reins. Ethan and Granger mounted their horses, and they headed for the ranch.


TAGGART DROVE THE buckboard right to the front door, and when the lieutenant stepped down, he took it over to the stable. Ethan dismounted, gave Granger his horse's reins. Granger followed the buckboard to the barn.

"Let's get you settled," Ethan said to Brodie.

As they entered the house Moze stepped forward.

"Moze will show you to your room," Ethan said. "When you come down we'll have a drink, and then some lunch."

"I'll take your bag, suh," Moze said.

"Thank you both," Brodie said. He followed Moze up the stairs.

Ethan was having a drink, sitting in his leather chair, when Moze came down.

"I put him in a room and made sure he had water to freshen up with, Cap'n."

"Good, Moze."

"Now I'll go and sees to lunch."

"Is it somethin' good?" Ethan asked.

Moze grinned and said, "Not as good as supper gon' be."

"You're a good man, Moze."

"Suh."

Moze went to the kitchen and Ethan drank his whiskey and waited. He wasn't sure what to expect from Brodie, who so far had been very genial, almost too . . . affable.

Brodie didn't waste any time coming back down. He looked like he'd washed and changed his tunic.

"Whiskey?" Ethan offered, standing up.

"Sounds good, Captain," Brodie said.

As Ethan carried the drink to Brodie and handed it to him he said, "I told you, I'm not a Captain anymore."

"You earned that rank, sir," Brodie said. "I don't think that goes away, do you?"

"Not sure I agree with that, Lieutenant," Ethan said. "By the way, what's your first name?"

"Oh, sorry," Brodie said. "I didn't introduce myself properly when I got off the stage. I'm Lieutenant Francis S. Brodie. Those who know me best call me Frank."

At that point Moze appeared in the doorway.

"Lunch is served, suhs," he said.

"Lieutenant," Ethan said, "take your drink with you."

"And after lunch can we take a look at some stock?" Brodie asked, as they walked.

"By all means," Ethan said.

"I saw some of them in the corral as we arrived," Brodie said. "Good-looking animals."

"We like 'em."

As they reached the table Brodie saw that it was set for two.

"Your foreman and the sergeant won't be joining us?" he asked.

"They will for supper," Ethan said. "I just thought you might be hungry when you got off the stage. I told Moze to put a little something together."

Brodie eyed the plates of food on the table and said, "This is a little something?"

"Wait till you see what he does for supper," Ethan said, as they sat. "Dig in, Lieutenant."

IN THE BARN while Taggart unhitched the team from the buckboard and Granger unsaddled the horses, the two men discussed the newcomer.

"What d'ya think, Sarge?" Taggart asked.

"He makes me antsy," Granger said. "He's too damn . . . what's the word?"

"Nice?"

"That's it," Granger said. "I ain't never met an officer that nice."

"You think he's tryin' to pull somethin'?"

"If he is, Ethan ain't gonna fall for it," Granger said.

"I agree with you, there," Taggart said. "The Captain won't let 'im get away with nothin'."

"Ethan's gonna give 'im lunch," Granger said. "We got time. Let's make sure those horses in the corral are ready."

"Yeah, you never know when one of 'em is gonna go lame," Taggart said.

They finished what they were doing and headed for the corral.

AFTER LUNCH ETHAN and Brodie left the house and walked over to the corral, where Granger and Taggart were waiting. They both gave Ethan a nod, meaning the horses were looking good.

"Mind if I go in?" Brodie asked.

"Be my guest," Ethan said, and Taggart opened the gate for him.

When Ethan watched Brodie in among the horses, interacting with them with ease, checking hooves, teeth and eyes, he started to respect him as a horseman. Now it remained to be seen what kind of negotiator he would turn out to be.

"He knows what he's doin'," Granger mumbled to Ethan.

"That must be why the quartermaster sent him," Ethan said.

Brodie finished up his inspection and came out of the corral, where he faced Ethan, Taggart, and Granger.

"I don't see anything wrong with these animals," he said.

"Then we can talk price?" Ethan asked.

"Oh, not yet," the man said. "Where are the rest of the herd?"

"The herd is in the Big Valley Meadow," Ethan said. "These were just to give you an idea of the quality."

"Well, the quality of these is good," Brodie said, "no doubt about it, but this is just twenty. I can't make an offer on two hundred based on the condition of twenty. I have to see the herd."

"That's gonna take you some time," Ethan said. "We'll have to ride out there early tomorrow."

"That suits me," the lieutenant said. "If they're as good as these, I'm looking forward to it."

"The whole herd is like these," Taggart assured him.

"No offense," Brodie said, "but I've got to see for myself, if you don't mind."

"We don't mind at all," Ethan said, before either of the other two men could comment.

# CHAPTER SEVEN

OVER SUPPER BRODIE chattered on while Ethan, Granger, and Taggart ate and listened. Turned out the man had gotten his lieutenant's promotion on the battlefield. They also discovered that he liked talking about himself.

Moze brought out some more chicken and Brodie said, "This is the best meal I've had since—well, lunch."

"I's glad you likes it, suh," Moze said.

As Moze went into the kitchen Brodie asked, "You brought one of the freed slaves here with you?"

"Moze was a free man during the war," Ethan said. "He joined up, and ended up in my unit. He's a good man, and agreed to come here and work with me."

"Seems like quite a few of your men did that," Brodie said, looking at Taggart and Granger.

"You don't know the half of it," Taggart said. "Every man on this ranch served with the Captain during the war."

"I see," Brodie said. "That's a lot of loyalty, Captain."

"I prefer to think of it as friendship."

"Really?" Brodie said. "But aren't you paying them?"

"Yes," Ethan said, "every man is being paid."

"When you said friendship I thought you meant they were working here for free."

"Like we fought the war for Mr. Lincoln for free?" Granger demanded.

"Every soldier was paid a salary," Brodie said.

"If you can call what we got a salary," Taggart said.

"You were clothed and fed, as well," Brodie pointed out.

"If you can call that fed," Granger said.

"Okay, okay," Ethan said, "we're gettin' off the subject. We should be talkin' horses."

"There's not much more to talk about until I see the entire herd," Brodie said.

"And are you authorized to make a deal?" Ethan asked. "I'd like to get this drive going—"

"I'm authorized," Brodie said, "but once we agree on a price, we'll need those horses to be in Fort Davis in forty-five days."

"Forty-five days?" Taggart blurted. "Are you nuts? Fort Davis is in Texas."

"I know where Fort Davis is, Mr. Taggart," Brodie said.

"Then you know what you're askin' is impossible," Granger said. "Does Ethan gettin' paid depend on that timetable?"

"It does."

"So what do you intend to do—what does the army intend to do—if we get there in, say, forty-seven days?" Taggart asked.

"It's very simple," Brodie said. "If you can't get there in forty-five days, there's no deal."

"So the army needs horses," Granger said, "unless

we don't get there in that time period. Then . . . what? You don't need them, anymore?"

"What are we supposed to do with two hundred horses if we get to Fort Davis and they don't accept delivery and pay us?"

Brodie drank some water before answering.

"I suspect they'll try to make a new deal," he said.

Both Granger and Taggart stared at Brodie, then looked at Ethan.

"You see what they're doin'?" Granger asked. "They're givin' us an impossible deadline, and when we get there late they'll cut the price."

"That's the army, for you," Taggart hissed.

"Captain," Brodie said, rising, "think it over and in the morning let me know if we'll be going to see the herd. Good night, gentlemen."

Brodie left the room. All three of them listened to him ascend the stairs.

"Ethan, you can't—" Granger started.

"They're tryin' to steal—" Taggart said.

"Stop!" Ethan told them.

Both men fell silent.

"Let's deal with things as they come," Ethan said. "Brodie seems to know his horseflesh. He can see that our horses are worth the price we're askin'."

"And what if he was told to dicker?" Taggart said. "To get the horses cheaper?"

"Like I said," Ethan replied, "we'll handle that if and when the time comes. Now, finish eatin' and get out. I want some quiet time to think."

Granger and Taggart left the last bits of their cobbler and said good-night.

Outside, on the porch, Granger said, "Time to think. He *is* worried that the army's gonna try to undercut us."

"You can't trust an officer," Taggart said.

"Well," Granger said, "Ethan's gonna have to handle it."

"If anybody can, it's him," Taggart said.

"All we have to do is stay ready to back his play," Granger said. "You know, I'm surprised they sent this lieutenant here alone."

"I was thinkin' that too, when he got off the stage," Taggart said.

"Somethin' ain't right, here," Granger said. "We definitely gotta have the boss's back on this one."

"We will," Taggart said, "we're gonna have to back whatever play he makes, no questions asked."

IN THE HOUSE Ethan sat in his chair with a glass of whiskey and a cigar. He alternated sipping the liquid and drawing from the cigar. He blew smoke out slowly so that it billowed in front of him, and he stared into it, looking for answers. Instead, what he saw in the smoke was the battlefield. No battle in particular, just an amalgam of all of them, his men being chopped to pieces by bullets and bayonets. It was something he usually saw in his sleep, not when he was awake. But Lieutenant Brodie was in his house, representing the army, stirring up bad memories.

He looked up when he heard a board creak on the stairs. Then Lieutenant Brodie appeared in the doorway.

"Your men are gone?" he asked.

"Turned in for the night."

He entered the room.

"They don't like me, much."

"They don't like the army much, Lieutenant," Ethan said. "It's nothin' personal. Whiskey?"

"Sure."

"Help yourself," Ethan said. "It's right over there."

Brodie walked over and poured himself a shot.

"Have a seat," Ethan invited.

"What about you?" Brodie asked, sitting on the sofa. "What do you think of the army?"

"I didn't enjoy myself while I was there," Ethan said. "And now I'm only dealin' with them out of necessity."

Brodie sipped his whiskey.

"If I could've sold my horses to somebody else, I would've," Ethan admitted.

"I'm not here to try to cheat you, Captain," Brodie told him.

"Oh, I know," Ethan said. "You're just here to do your job. That's what we're all doin', you know. Our jobs."

Brodie finished his whiskey, set the glass down on the table next to the sofa.

"Well, thanks for the drink," he said, standing. "I think I'll probably sleep now."

"Now that you had a drink," Ethan said, "or now that we talked?"

Brodie smiled.

"A little of both, I guess. Good night, Captain."

"Good night, Lieutenant."

Brodie left the room and later Ethan heard the board creak again. Moments later, Moze appeared in the doorway.

"You need anythin', suh?"

"I need a dose of Moze, my friend," Ethan said. "Have a drink with me."

"Yessuh."

He started for the bottle, but Ethan stood and said, "I'll get it. Siddown."

"Yessuh."

Moze went and sat on the sofa. Ethan poured himself another whiskey, and one for Moze, then carried it to the old Black man.

"Thank yuh, suh," Moze said, accepting it.

Ethan went back to his chair.

"You heard everythin' that's been said, haven't you, Moze?" Ethan said.

"Ah don't eavesdrop, suh."

"I didn't say you did," Ethan replied. "I just know you've got big ears, my friend. Goin' all the way back to the war."

"Well . . ." Moze said, and sipped his whiskey.

"What do you think of Lieutenant Brodie?"

"He's a soldier, suh."

"And?"

"If'n you don't mind me sayin' so, suh," Moze said, "he's too damn polite."

"I don't mind you sayin' so, at all, Moze," Ethan said. "That's why I asked. I knew you'd be honest. I know you have a habit of seein' the truth."

"Yessuh," Moze said, "ever since I was younger."

"You think he's gonna try to cheat me for the army?" Ethan asked.

"I sure do, boss," Moze said. "But it's like you told Mistuh Taggart and Mistuh Granger, he's here ta do his job, and you is gonna hafta do yours."

"So we just all do our jobs," Ethan said, "and see who comes out on top."

"Yessuh," Moze said, "but if'n you don't mind me sayin' so, suh, I gots faith in you. I think you is the one gonna come out on top."

Ethan smiled.

"You know, Moze," he said, "I think that's probably what I wanted to hear." He put his empty glass on the table next to his chair. "I think I'll turn in now."

"I take care of these here glasses before I turns in," Moze promised.

"Thanks, Moze. Good night."

"Night, Cap'n."

* * *

IN HIS ROOM Lieutenant Frank Brodie stripped down to his skivvies, then walked to the window and looked out over the Paradise Ranch. He could see the corral of horses, and the barn in the moonlight. He had heard many stories about Captain Ethan Miller, and he was thinking they were probably all true. The man watched him like a hawk whenever they were in a room together. It gave Brodie the heebie-jeebies. It was like the man was looking right through him.

And the others, Granger and Taggart, they didn't trust him as far as they could throw him. But he had been sent on this assignment because he knew horses, and he knew men. He had wanted a man to come with him—an adjutant, perhaps—but he had been sent alone.

"Miller's not going to like you," he was told, "because you're Army. There's no point in rubbing his face in the uniform. You handle this alone, Lieutenant. It'll be a feather in your cap."

No promise of a promotion, just a goddamn feather in his cap. There were times he could commiserate with Captain Miller for the way he felt about the army. Brodie had been in the military over twenty years, and he was still a lieutenant, a rank he had been stuck at for ten years.

He stepped away from the window and got into bed. As he was falling asleep he thought, when this was over, maybe Captain Miller could use another hand.

# CHAPTER EIGHT

Ⅰ N THE MORNING Abraham made breakfast for Ethan and Lieutenant Brodie. Granger and Taggart had breakfast in the mess with the rest of the men.

"Are you gonna want to pick out your own horse?" Ethan asked Brodie.

"I'm sure whatever you have for me will be fine, Captain."

"You finish your coffee, then," Ethan said, standing up, "and I'll have the horses saddled. Come out when you're done."

"Thanks, Captain."

Ethan left and Moze came out of the kitchen.

"Think I can get some more coffee, boy?" Brodie asked.

"I ain't been called 'boy' since the war," Moze said. "The war's over, ain't it, suh?"

"Yeah, it is," Brodie said. "I'm sorry. It's Moze, right?"

"That's right, suh."

"Can I get some more coffee, Moze?"

"Sure t'ing, Lieutenant."

Moze got the pot and poured Brodie another cup.

"Thanks, Moze," Brodie said. "You like working for Captain Miller, don't you?"

"Oh, yessuh," Moze said. "He's a good man. He takes care of his own."

"His own?"

"His men," Moze said. "Every man on this ranch served with him in the war."

"So I heard," Brodie said. "He's a good boss?"

"He was a good commander," Moze said, "and he a good boss, yessuh."

"What do you think—"

"I gots to get back to the kitchen now, suh," Moze said. "Can I get you anythin' else?"

"No, thanks," Brodie said. "This'll do it."

Moze went back into the kitchen, and Brodie finished his coffee.

WHEN ETHAN GOT to the barn he found Granger and another man there, saddling horses.

"Mornin', boss," Granger said, and the other man waved.

"Mornin'," Ethan said. "How many men we takin' with us this mornin'?"

"Just me, Taggart, and two others to spell the two who are out there. We been guardin' that herd day and night."

"Good thinkin'," Ethan said. "I'm gonna saddle my horse, and one for Brodie. I think that palomino in the corral will suit him."

"I'll get it, boss," the other man, Pickett, said.

"Thanks, Hank," Ethan said.

He started to saddle his own horse, a five-year-old

roan, and then Pickett brought in the palomino and he saddled that one with a spare saddle they kept in the barn. By the time Ethan had finished, Granger and Pickett had saddled the other four horses, and walked them all out.

Taggart was coming over from the bunkhouse with another man named Franklin, and Brodie was coming from the house.

"Which one's mine?" Brodie asked.

"The palomino," Ethan told him.

"Well," Brodie said, "trying to impress me, huh?"

The other six men all mounted up and waited while Brodie ran his hands over the palomino's flanks.

"So?" Ethan said.

"It'll do," Brodie said, with a grin. "Thanks, Captain."

He mounted up, and Ethan followed.

"Where are we headed?" Brodie asked.

"Big Sky Meadow," Ethan said.

"Okay," Brodie said, "lead the way."


WHEN THEY REACHED the meadow the two hands who were on guard all night rode up to meet them.

"Mornin', boss," one of them said.

"You two can go back to the ranch and get some sleep," Ethan said. "We'll take it from here."

"Sure thing, boss," the other man said, and they rode off.

"Well," Ethan said to Brodie, "there they are." The herd was stretched out in front of them. "You wanna go down and check each one?"

"I think a short ride for a quick look-see should do it," Brodie said.

"Fine," Ethan said, "go ahead."

"I'll go with 'im," Taggart said, "in case he's got any questions."

"Let's go, Mr. Taggart," Brodie said, and kicked his heels into the palomino. Taggart urged his paint to follow.

Ethan looked at Pickett and Franklin and said, "We'll be out of here in no time. You boys hang back and keep an eye on the herd. You'll be spelled later today."

"Sure, boss," Pickett said.

"When do ya think we'll start the drive, boss?" Franklin asked.

"The lieutenant and me, we'll be goin' back to the house to talk price. I get what I want, we'll be drivin' them out of here in a couple of days."

"Sounds good," Pickett said.

The two men turned their horses and rode down toward the herd.

"You think you're gonna get your price?" Granger asked.

"I don't know," Ethan said. "He's kinda hard to read."

"Which is probably why they sent him," Granger said. "To throw you off."

"We'll see who gets thrown off," Ethan said.

While they watched, Brodie rode around the outskirts of the herd. Some of the horses got skittish, but the man seemed to know what he was doing. He backed off when he needed to, and he never dismounted. Eventually, he rode back up to where Ethan was waiting, with Taggart coming behind him.

"Good-lookin' animals, right?" Granger asked.

Brodie didn't answer. Instead he said, "I think I've seen enough. We can go back to the house and talk, Captain."

"Okay," Ethan said, "just let me and my foreman give my men some instructions. George?"

Ethan and Taggart rode toward the herd, heading for Pickett and Franklin.

"Did he say anythin'?" Ethan asked.

"Not a word to me," Taggart said, "but while he was ridin' around the herd it looked like he was talkin'."

"To who?"

"Himself?" Taggart said. "The horses? I don't know."

"All right." Ethan looked up toward Brodie and Granger. "He's watchin' us. Let's talk to the men and then go."

They rode over to their two men and told them they were leaving.

"Keep a sharp eye out," Ethan said. He was always afraid they would have to deal with rustlers. There was no indication that there were any in the vicinity, but he kept his men on alert.

"You got it, boss," Pickett said. "I hope you get your price."

"Yeah, me too, partner," Ethan said.

He and Taggart turned their horses and rode back up to Brodie and Granger.

"Everything okay?" Brodie asked.

"Fine," Ethan said. "I'm just always on the lookout for rustlers." He turned to Granger. "Let's head back."

"Right," Granger said.

"Have you seen any rustlers?" Brodie asked.

"No," Ethan said, "but that doesn't mean they're not out there."

"Then don't you think you should have more than two men out here on watch?"

"You might be right," Ethan said.

"If this is going to be the US Army's herd, I want them kept safe," Brodie said.

"They're not yours yet."

"It's just a matter of dickering," Brodie said.

Ethan studied the man, then said, "I'll send four more men out as soon as we get back."

"Good," Brodie said. "Then we can talk price."

Even though Brodie was talking like the herd was already the army's, Ethan still wasn't sure the deal was going to go through. He would have to figure just how far he could come down in price and still come out of this close to the way he wanted.

W HEN THEY GOT back to the ranch they all dismounted, and Ethan handed Taggart the reins of his and Brodie's horses.

"Send four more men out to the herd," Ethan said. "For the rest of the time Brodie's here, I want half a dozen men on watch."

"Are you thinkin' the army might try to steal the herd?" Taggart said.

"Probably not. The extra men are his idea."

"Okay, boss, I'll take care of it."

As Ethan walked away he heard his foreman telling Pickett and Franklin to unsaddle the horses. Then Taggart and Granger headed for the bunkhouse. Ethan caught up with Brodie and they walked to the house.

W HAT'S GOIN' ON?" Granger asked Taggart.

"The boss wants six men on the herd from now on," Taggart said.

"Is he thinkin' rustlers?" Granger asked. "Or does he think the army—could Brodie be here in advance of the army rustlin' the herd?"

"Not sure," Taggart said, "but they'd never get away with it. And the boss says the extra men on watch are Lieutenant Brodie's idea."

"Okay, but let's make sure they're well armed," Granger said.

"Agreed," Taggart said, as they reached the bunkhouse together.

\* \* \*

Ethan led Brodie into the sitting room, poured two whiskeys, and handed the man one. Could it be possible that Brodie was an advance scout for a party of rustlers? The telegram from the US Army said a Lieutenant Francis Brodie would be arriving, but he could have been intercepted and this man substituted for him.

Ethan went to his desk, opened the top drawer and took out a pistol. He pointed it at Brodie.

"Whoa!" the man said. "What's this?"

"I need you to take your gun out and toss it aside . . . now!"

Brodie undid the flap on his holster and obeyed, tossing his weapon away.

"It occurs to me I haven't seen your bona fides, Lieutenant," Ethan said.

"My what?"

"I don't know that you're really Lieutenant Francis Brodie," Ethan said. "I'm afraid before we go any further, I'm gonna need some proof."

# CHAPTER NINE

Y OU'RE BEING PARANOID, Captain," Brodie said.

"Not really," Ethan said. "You keep callin' me Captain. Well, I'm a little out of practice being a soldier. I should have asked you this the moment you got off the stage."

"I'll have to go upstairs and get my paperwork," Brodie said.

"Why don't we do that together?"

Ethan followed Brodie up to his room, where the soldier got some papers out of his carpetbag. He turned, as if to hand them to Ethan, who waved him off.

"Let's go downstairs," Ethan said. "I'll look at them there."

They went back down, and Ethan told Brodie to sit on the sofa. Then, holding his gun in one hand and the paperwork in the other, he examined it.

"Well?"

"Your orders seem valid," Ethan said, putting them

aside, "but I still don't know that you are really— well, you."

"Then what do you suggest we do next?"

"I'm gonna send a man to town to send a dispatch to the army for your description," Ethan said. "While we wait, we can talk price."

"Well, all right," Brodie said. "I guess I can't blame you for being careful."

"Moze!"

When the Black man came running in Ethan told him what he wanted to do.

"Go and tell Taggart to send somebody to town, now," Ethan said.

"Yessuh."

"And tell them not to come back without a reply."

"Yessuh."

As Moze left, Brodie said, "Washington may not get back to you that fast."

"If the army wants their horses, they will," Ethan said. He tucked his gun in his belt.

"You're not going to hold me at gunpoint?"

"There's no need," Ethan said. "You don't have your gun, and we're just going to talk price. Of course, if you try something—"

"I have nothing to try, Captain," Brodie said. "Let's talk business."


THEY SAT AT Ethan's desk, across from each other, and talked. As they had all suspected, Brodie started by trying to whittle Ethan's price down.

"Come on, Captain," he said, "we're talking two hundred head."

"If you take the whole herd," Ethan said.

"Would you sell part of it?"

"No," Ethan said. "All or nothing."

"Can you afford for it to be nothing?"

"Come on, Lieutenant," Ethan said. "Your bosses told you how much they're willing to pay. Don't try to impress them by getting the price down lower."

"I'm just doing my job, Captain."

They went back to talking price . . .


THEY BROKE FOR supper, which Moze put out on the table for the two of them.

"What about Granger and Taggart?" Brodie asked.

"They'll eat with the men."

"Are those pork chops?"

"I butchered a pig," Moze said, putting a platter of steaming vegetables on the table.

"It looks great."

Ethan and Brodie ate in silence, each planning out their next argument. As they were finishing up the front door opened and Taggart came walking in.

"Got it," he said.

He walked to the table and handed Ethan a telegram. Ethan took his gun from his belt and set it on the table.

"What's that for?"

"If you're not Brodie," Ethan said, "I'm going to shoot you."

"Kill me?"

"That depends," Ethan said. He read the telegram looked at Brodie, read it again, then took the gun and slid it back into his belt.

"Am I me?" Brodie asked.

"It looks like it," Ethan said.

Brodie breathed a sigh of relief.

"But your CO says there's a question you can answer," Ethan said.

"Oh, yeah?" Brodie asked. "What's that?"

"What's your wife's sister's name?"

"My wife's sister?"

"That's right," Ethan said. "It's right here."

Brodie grinned.

"There's no name there," he said, "because not only doesn't my wife have a sister, I don't have a wife."

Ethan looked at Taggart.

"Have you eaten?"

"No," Taggart said, "I went to town myself."

"Moze!"

"Yessuh," Moze said, sticking his head out the door.

"Set a plate out for Taggart," Ethan said. "Lieutenant Brodie and me are going back to the front room."

"Yessuh. Will you take coffee there?"

"Yes."

Ethan and Brodie stood up.

"Sit down and eat, Taggart," Ethan said. "And take your time."

"Yes, *sir*!"

Ethan led the way back to the front room, where he and Brodie once again sat with his desk between them.

"Can I have my gun back?" Brodie asked.

"When we're done here," Ethan said. "I don't think you're gonna be needin' it, do you?"

THEY CONTINUED TO negotiate into the night, neither wanting to give an inch. Taggart finished eating and left. Moze kept bringing coffee refills, and eventually they started putting whiskey into the cups as well.

Brodie stood up at one point and stretched.

"I think we might have to put this off until tomorrow," he said.

"That'll put me another day behind," Ethan said.

"It doesn't matter what day you leave," Brodie reminded him. "You have forty-five days from that point to deliver the herd."

"And you're eventually gonna make me a lump sum offer on the entire herd, right?" Ethan asked "After draggin' me all through this?".

"And what about you?" Brodie asked. "You got a lump sum offer for me?"

"Sit down," Ethan said.

Brodie sat.

Ethan got two pieces of paper and two pencils, passed one of each to Brodie.

"Write down a number, Lieutenant," he said. "Let's get this over with."

"All right."

They each wrote a number down on their slip of paper.

"This is my final offer," Brodie said.

"Same here," Ethan said. "If we don't agree on this, I'm gonna hafta look elsewhere for another buyer, and you're gonna have to explain to the army why they didn't get their horses."

Brodie looked at Ethan, gauging whether or not he was telling the truth. Finally he made an annoyed face. He crossed out the number he had written, and wrote down another. Only then did he exchange papers with Ethan.

They each unfolded the paper and read the number the other had written. Ethan could see the first number Brodie wrote down. It was one he would have rejected. Instead, he stood up and offered Brodie his hand.

Brodie stood up and shook it.

"You got yourself a herd, Lieutenant Brodie," Ethan said.

"Drink?" Ethan asked.

"Without the coffee?" Brodie asked.

"Straight whiskey."

"Yes, *sir.*"

M AJOR BENJAMIN DONOVAN, commanding officer of the Quartermaster's Office, entered the White House office of the President of the United States, and sat on a sofa.

"The president will be in shortly," he was told.

"Thank you."

It was fifteen minutes before a door opened and Ulysses S. Grant entered the room.

"Major," he said, walking to his desk.

"Mr. President!" Donovan said, jumping to his feet.

"Have a seat over here, Major, in front of my desk," Grant said, while lighting a huge cigar.

"Yes, sir."

Donovan crossed the room and sat facing the President.

"Sonsofbitches!" Grant swore. "I've got a unit of graybacks in Texas who won't accept that Lee surrendered."

"What are you going to do, sir?"

"I'm sending Phil Sheridan in to clean them out," Grant said.

"Yessir, very good sir."

"But that's not why you're here, Major," Grant said. "Tell me."

"I haven't heard anything yet, sir," the major said, "but we did get a telegram from Ethan Miller, wanting to check the credentials of one Lieutenant Francis Brodie."

"And you sent confirmation, of course."

"Yessir," Donovan said, "a description and a key question."

"Good, good," Grant said. "We need that herd, Major. I hope you told your man not to try and play it cute with a man like Ethan Miller."

"Uh, yes, sir, I told him to be, uh, aware of Miller's background."

"He was a damned good soldier," Grant said. "I got glowing reports from Phil Sheridan. I wanted to promote him after the war, but he refused and mustered out."

"Really, sir?"

"Bought a spread of his own, and look where we are now. About to do business with each other."

"Yes, sir."

"I wanna know as soon as you hear from your man, Major," Grant said, waving the cigar.

"Oh, you will, sir," the major said. "I'll come right over myself."

"See to it that you do," Grant said. "You're dismissed."

"Yes, sir."

Major Donovan, sweating under his arms, turned and left the President's Office.

President Grant sat back in his chair and puffed on his cigar, filling the air with the acrid smoke. He just hoped Phil Sheridan was right about former Captain Ethan Miller.

# CHAPTER TEN

T HE NEXT MORNING Ethan and Brodie rode into
Bozeman. The lieutenant went into the bank, and
Ethan waited outside. Brodie came out in fifteen
minutes.

"You want to do this here?" he asked.

"Let's get a cup of coffee."

They walked a couple of blocks until they came to
the Tumbleweed Café. They went inside, got seated,
and ordered coffee.

"If you want breakfast it might take a while," the
waiter said. "This is our rush time."

"Just the coffee," Ethan said.

"That I can do."

They waited until they each had a cup in front of
them before starting to talk.

"I've got some money in my pocket," Brodie said.

"A down payment?" Ethan asked.

"Let's call it expense money, to help you get outfitted," Brodie said. "If you don't make it in forty-five

days we don't want it to be because you weren't properly outfitted."

"We'll make it in forty-five days."

"Are you sure?" Brodie asked. "Look, this deadline wasn't my idea. In fact, I was against it. But I wasn't in on the decision-making process."

"That's what I figured."

"So you know the dickering, the deadline, it's all to make you fail so they can really get the price down when you get there."

"I knew that," Ethan said, "but I didn't think you'd admit it."

"I told you," Brodie said, "none of this was my idea. So let's go back to your ranch to sign the contract, and I'll give you your expense money."

"I'm surprised the army is even comin' up with that," Ethan said.

"Okay," Brodie said, as they stood to leave, "I've got to admit, that was my idea."

They left the café and walked to where they had left their horses.

"When are you headin' back?" Ethan asked, as they mounted up.

"I'm leavin' tomorrow," Brodie said.

"We'll leave the day after," Ethan said. "I'll use tomorrow to spend some of that expense money."

"I'll make a note of the date when the forty-five-day clock starts," Brodie said.


W HEN THEY GOT back to the house Ethan asked Taggart and Granger to come inside and witness the contract. The four of them gathered around the desk and Brodie spread the papers out on the desk. Ethan hated to admit it, but the numbers he and Brodie had agreed on were already on the contract.

Ethan let his foreman and top hand look the paperwork over, and then he and Brodie signed.

"Forty-five days," Brodie said, "starting the day after tomorrow."

"What are we gonna do tomorrow?" Taggart asked.

Brodie dropped a stack of bills on the desk.

"George, you take that money to town tomorrow and get us what we'll need for the trip," Ethan said.

"Right," Taggart said. "I'll talk to Abraham and Moze and see what they need for the chuck wagon."

"Nice to know your priorities are in the right place," Ethan said. "Bill, tomorrow you sit the men down and explain what's expected of them."

"That nobody falls off their horse," Granger said.

"You sound like you've got everything planned," Brodie said. "I guess I'll just stay out of your hair the rest of today. My stage leaves at ten tomorrow morning."

"You can ride into town with Taggart," Ethan said.

"My pleasure," Taggart said, sarcastically.

"And keep six men on the herd at all times," Ethan said. "Last thing we need is to be rustled just before our trip."

"We haven't seen any signs," Granger said, "and haven't heard anythin' in town."

"Just to be on the safe side," Ethan said.

"Right."

Taggart and Granger left and Ethan filed the contract away in his desk.

"Drink?" Ethan asked.

"Always," Brodie said.

Ethan poured two whiskeys and handed Brodie one.

"Here's to your drive," Brodie said. "May it be smooth going."

"I'll drink to that," Ethan said, "but it ain't likely. There are always problems, we just have to hope we can handle them all."

"You've got a good foreman, good top hand," Brodie said. "I assume you have good men."

"I do."

"Then you should make it," Brodie said. "If you don't do it in forty-five days, you'll still get paid, you'll just have to renegotiate the price."

"I can't sell this herd any cheaper," Ethan said. "I've got to be able to pay my men and keep my ranch going."

"Your original deal would have enabled you to do that, eh?" Brodie asked.

"Easily."

"And it was with a circus?"

"They were gonna buy the horses and then take their show to Europe," Ethan said.

"What happened?"

"I don't know," Ethan said. "I just got a telegram that said 'things changed.'"

"And that's when you contacted the military?"

"There was nothin' else I could do," Ethan said. "Findin' another private buyer could've taken weeks, maybe months. These horses would be skin and bones by then."

"Crow bait."

"Exactly."

"Well," Brodie said, "I doubt you're going to let that happen, Captain."

"I'm gonna do my best."

"Well, I'm going up to my room," Brodie said, setting his empty glass down. "I'll be down for supper, though. One last meal of Abraham's."

"I'll tell 'im to make it special," Ethan said.

Brodie nodded, and left the room. Ethan heard the creaking step as the soldier went up the stairs.

Ethan poured himself another drink and sat in his chair. *Forty-five days,* he thought, *is gonna be a bitch.*

\* \* \*

AFTER A WHILE Ethan decided to go out to the barn and check on his roan, make sure the horse was in shape for the drive. While each of the hands had their own animals, he was also going to have to pick out the horses for the remuda. The hands would probably be changing mounts three or four times a day, which meant the important position on the drive would be the wrangler. Ethan wanted to talk with Taggart about that.

When he got to the barn it was empty, but he knew the next day—the day before the drive—each of the hands would be checking on their own mounts. It would be up to Ethan and his foreman which horses would be in the remuda.

But for now, Ethan gave his full attention to his roan. The animal had been fine on the ride into town and back, but the drive would be grueling, and he had to make sure the roan was fit.

He was giving the animal a thorough examination when Granger came walking in.

"We had the same idea," he said. "I want to check out my paint."

Ethan looked over at Granger's horse, a six-year-old. Paints were known for their athleticism and strength.

"He looks good," Ethan said.

"I'll just make sure."

While they were checking their horses, Taggart came in.

"Same idea?" he said, walking over to the stall with his Appaloosa, which was also known for its stamina and strength.

"You talk to the men?" Ethan asked.

"They're all set," Taggart said.

"Do you have somebody in mind for the wrangler?" Ethan asked.

"Stackhouse," Taggart said. "If you remember during the war he usually handled the horses."

"I do remember," Ethan said. "He'll do."

"What about the horses?" Granger asked.

"Me and Taggart'll take Stackhouse and we'll pick them out," Ethan said.

"What about Brodie?" Granger said. "What's he gonna do?"

"He's in his room," Ethan said. "He's gonna come down for supper. You two can join us, if you want."

"Why not?" Granger said. "Abraham makin' somethin' special?"

"He is."

"Might as well," Taggart said, "before we start eatin' trail rations."

"Moze and Abraham can do wonders with a chuck wagon," Ethan said.

"Yeah, maybe," Taggart said. "Still . . ."

Ethan, satisfied with the condition of his horse, said, "All right, then. I'll see you both tonight for supper. Make it six."

"Right," Granger said.

"And tell Stackhouse to be ready tomorrow mornin'," Ethan said. "I want to get the remuda set up first thing."

"Right, boss," Taggart said.

He left the two men running their hands over their horses' legs and flanks.

B RODIE SAT IN his room, hoping he had done the right thing confiding in Miller. He looked out his window, saw Ethan walking to the barn. The man had been a good soldier, but when the war ended he'd had enough. Brodie knew General Phil Sheridan wanted to keep Miller in the service and promote him, but Captain Miller wouldn't have it. Then, when the military got Miller's telegram, they saw a way to get him back in.

Brodie didn't know if this was going to work. But he had done his part, his duty. Tomorrow he would head back to Washington. Maybe he would hear how this played out, and maybe not. Once his job was done, he was out of it, and nobody was going to see that he was kept informed.

He respected Ethan Miller, even thought about joining him on the drive, but in the end he was a soldier. He had done what he'd been ordered to do, and now he had to go back.

He saw Granger, and then Taggart go into the barn. Ethan come walking back. Their loyalty to him was further indication of the kind of man Ethan Miller was.

Finally, when it was late enough, he left his room to go down to his last supper with Miller and his men.

# CHAPTER ELEVEN

MOZE GAVE BRODIE some breakfast before he left. Once he was gone, Ethan went and had breakfast with the men. Taggart and one other man, Costigan, were the only ones missing. They had taken a buckboard into town, driving Brodie to the train station, after which they would pick up supplies for the drive.

With the forty-five-day clock starting the next day, Ethan would have liked to get started a day early, but it just wasn't possible. Moze and Abraham needed the day to put the chuck wagon together, while Ethan and Stackhouse assembled the remuda.

They had half the horses picked out when Abraham called out that lunch was ready. Taggart and Costigan weren't back from town yet.

Once again, Ethan ate with the crew. Over lunch he and Stackhouse discussed the rest of the horses. The men who weren't guarding the herd discussed what the drive was going to be like. Only a few of them had ever been on a drive before the war, and none since. But they had all been in training since coming to Paradise with Ethan. Still, they wouldn't know how difficult a task the drive would be until they started.

"Okay," Ethan said, pushing his plate away, "let's go, Stack. Let's get this finished." He stood up and raised his voice. "The rest of you finish lunch and get your kits together, then go out and relieve the others so they can do the same."

"Yes, sir," one man said, for all of them.

Ethan and Stackhouse went back to the corral. As they got there, the buckboard pulled up and Taggart and Costigan stepped down.

"Go get some lunch," Ethan told Costigan, "then get your kit together for the drive."

"Yes, sir."

Ethan looked at Taggart.

"Brodie get on the stage?"

"Yeah," Taggart said. "I stayed there and waited till he boarded and the stage pulled away. He's gone."

"Did he say anythin' to you on the way to town?" Ethan asked.

"No," Taggart said. "He was quiet the whole way."

"Okay," Ethan said, "get Abraham to help you unload." Abraham was younger than Moze, who was too old for any heavy physical labor.

"I'll drive around to the back of the mess," Taggart said. That was where the chuck wagon was.

Ethan turned, saw that Stackhouse was in the corral. He joined him there.

B Y LATE AFTERNOON they had the entire remuda assembled.

"Go get yourself outfitted, Stack," Ethan said. "And tell Taggart and Granger I want them at the house."

"Yes, sir."

As Stackhouse headed for the bunkhouse, Ethan walked to the house. At the same time as he entered, Moze came out of the kitchen.

"How are things goin' with the chuck wagon?" Ethan asked.

"Abraham almost has it completely loaded, suh. To-morrow mornin' we'll load the last of the food."

"Fine."

"You wanna eat?" Moze asked.

"Yeah, sure," Ethan said. "Put out a spread for me, Taggart, and Granger. Is Abraham gonna have time to feed the men tonight?"

"Oh, yessuh," Moze said. "He gon' make them a fine supper for the night before we leave."

"Good," Ethan said. "I'm gonna get cleaned up."

"Supper be ready in an hour," Moze told him.

"Good. Thanks."

One of the things Ethan made sure the house had after he bought it was an indoor water closet, with a water pump. He went there and got washed up, then went to his bedroom and changed his clothes. By the time he came back down Taggart and Granger were there, waiting in the front sitting room.

"Ready to eat?" he asked.

"Starvin'," Taggart said. "I didn't get much lunch."

"I could eat," Granger said.

They went to the dining room, where Moze had covered the table with food.

"Did you leave anythin' in the pantry?" Ethan joked.

"Why?" Moze asked. "We's leavin' tomorrow."

"Good point," Ethan agreed. "Moze, why don't you sit and help us eat all this food?"

"Thank you, suh."

Ethan sat at the head of the table. Granger on his right, Taggart on his left. Moze sat down next to Taggart.

"Just to be clear," he said, while they ate. "We have forty-five days to make this drive, and deliver the horses. If we don't, the contract is no good, and I'll have to renegotiate."

"And they'll try to get the herd for a song," Granger said.

"Right. They'll know that I have to make a deal, or take a loss."

"Goddamn military," Taggart said.

"So we're gonna make that forty-five-day deadline," Ethan said. "No matter what."

"There's gonna be a lot of unanticipated problems, boss," Taggart said. He was one of the men who had trail drive experience before the war. "There always is."

"And we'll handle it," Ethan said. "Whatever comes along, we'll handle it." He looked at Moze. "Did you and Abraham leave room in the chuck wagon for extra guns?"

"Yessuh," Moze said.

Ethan looked at Taggart and Granger.

"After we eat I want to collect all the guns we can and pack them into that wagon. Got it?"

"Got it," Granger said. "You expectin' rustlers, after talkin' with Brodie?"

"Like I said," Ethan answered, "I wanna be ready for anythin'."

"Are we sure," Taggart said, "that the military won't try to take the herd from us along the way?"

"No," Ethan said, "we're not sure, but I don't think that'll happen. Brodie was pretty forthcoming with me. The military doesn't think we can deliver in forty-five days."

"So why try anythin' else?" Taggart said.

"Right."

"I'm not convinced," Granger said, "so I'll just wear

as many guns as I can without weighin' myself down too much."

"Sounds like a good idea," Taggart said.

"All right," Ethan said. "Tell all the men to do the same."

"You want I should wear a gun, boss?" Moze asked.

"Yeah, Moze, I do," Ethan said. "And tell Abraham to wear one."

"Yessuh."

They all stopped talking at that point and gave their attention to the spread Moze had prepared, which included chicken, beef, vegetables, and biscuits.

AFTER SUPPER TAGGART and Granger left the house. Moze started to clean the table, and Ethan began to help him.

"You don't hafta do that, suh," Moze said. "I got it."

"That's okay, Moze," Ethan said. "On this drive, we're all gonna hafta pitch in. I might as well start now."

"Yessuh."

They cleared the table, brought everything into the kitchen, scraped the remnants of the meal off the plates. At that point Ethan left Moze to wash everything and put it all away. None of it was going to be needed for months.

"Let me know when you're finished," Ethan said, "and we'll go over to the chuck wagon and load the extra weapons."

"Yessuh."

Ethan went to the sitting room, poured a whiskey, and sat at his desk. There was some paperwork he needed to finish so that it wouldn't be waiting for him when they got home. He was just finishing up when Moze appeared at the doorway.

"I's done, boss," the old Black man said.

Ethan looked up at him, saw something he didn't like. Moze looked tired.

"Moze, how old are you?"

"Suh?"

"I've never asked you that before," Ethan went on. "I always figured you were somewhere between forty and sixty. How close am I?"

"I's sixty-four, suh."

"Are you gonna be all right to make this drive?" Ethan asked.

"I's gon' be ridin' the chuck wagon, cookin' meals with Abraham, suh. I knows you said we's all gotta pitch in but you ain't gon' make me ride the herd, are ya?"

"No," Ethan said, "not that."

"Then I's be fine."

"Okay," Ethan said, "I'll take your word for it."


WHEN MOZE AND Ethan got to the chuck wagon, Taggart and Granger had already brought some guns to be loaded. Abraham was standing there, staring at the weapons, glassy-eyed. As they approached he looked up at them. Abraham had always appeared to be somewhere between forty and fifty, but now Ethan was thinking the man might be older than that.

"What's wrong, Abraham?" Ethan asked.

"Boss," Abraham said, "if you don' mind me sayin' so, I ain't gon' like havin' all dese guns in my wagon."

"I don't blame you," Ethan said, "but just to be on the safe side, I wanna have them with us, and I don't want to bring another wagon. Will they fit?"

"Dere's room," Abraham said. "I jus' don't like havin' all dese guns near my food."

"I understand, Abraham," Ethan said, "and I'm sorry."

"I's jus' sayin'," the Black man said.

"All right, then," Ethan said to Moze and Abraham, "let's get to work."

The three of them got the extra rifles and pistols loaded, and then Ethan left the two men to sort everything out and make it work.

Ethan walked over to the bunkhouse and entered. The men were being rowdy but quieted down when the boss entered.

"Who was on watch today?"

Six of the men raised their hands, which was pretty much every man there. Another six were out on night watch. The only ones missing were Granger and Taggart.

"See anybody?" he asked.

"No, sir," one man said. "We didn't see a thing."

"How's the herd?"

"They're fine, sir," another man said. "Standin' easy most of the day, just grazin'."

"Everybody get enough to eat?"

"Yes sir."

"I'm gonna ask you to go out and spell the others halfway through the night," Ethan said,. "I want everybody to get some sleep tonight. I can't have anybody stayin' up all night, and then startin' a drive."

"Yes, sir," the first man said. "We'll do that, Cap'n."

"This drive is gonna be a bitch," Ethan said, "and I wanna be on top of it right from the start."

"We understand Cap'n," another man said.

"Good," Ethan said. "Then I'll see all of you in the mornin'."

E THAN WOKE EARLY the next morning. Breakfast was to be a light, quick meal in the mess. He locked the house up tight. He wasn't leaving anyone behind to watch it, but Taggart had stopped in to see the sheriff in Bozeman, who promised to ride out every so often. He agreed to that because the Paradise was a prominent ranch in the county, and the lawman wouldn't mind having Ethan Miller beholden to him.

After breakfast Moze and Abraham got the horses hitched to the chuck wagon and drove it around to the front of the mess. Ethan, Taggart, Granger, and the hands all saddled their horses, and then Stackhouse and one other man drove the remuda out of the corral. The house, barn, bunkhouse, mess, and corral were now all empty.

Moze and Abraham climbed up onto the seat of the chuck wagon, and Abraham grabbed the reins.

"Are we ready?" Ethan called out.

Everybody agreed that they were.

"All right," Ethan shouted, "move out!"

They left the ranch and headed for Big Sky Meadow to pick up the herd.

# CHAPTER TWELVE

ETHAN WATCHED WHILE his men got the herd moving out of the meadow and heading south. They would start by driving them through Wyoming, then Colorado to New Mexico, where they would continue south and head for Texas. It was going to be a fourteen-hundred-mile drive, but the good part of it was that it was a straight run, with no changes in direction.

A typical cattle drive would probably cover about fifteen miles a day. Ethan figured he could get his horses to move faster than cattle. If they were going to make the forty-five-day deadline, they'd have to do at least thirty miles a day. The first few days would show them if it was even possible.

Ethan rode on the right flank with Taggart, while Granger rode the left with some of the other boys. Ethan left it to Taggart to decide who would ride drag, and then behind that the wrangler, Stackhouse, would be moving the remuda along with the help of one other man. He also left it to Taggart to assign a man to ride point, scouting ahead for problems so that they would see them coming.

The chuck wagon drove behind the remuda. Ethan wasn't really sure where the chuck wagon drove during a cattle drive. The wagon had only been invented by Colonel Charles Goodnight the year before. After Ethan read about Goodnight and his cattle drives, and the chuck wagon, he decided to put one together for Moze and Abraham. He didn't even know if they had done it right, but it was a wagon that was carrying food, and two men who would cook for the hands.

A few of the men had worked herds of horses before the war.

Ethan had taken the time to talk with them when he decided to drive the herd to market. He had been waiting for word from the circus, telling him where they wanted horses delivered. That word never came. But it was the military who decided they needed the horses, and they needed them for Fort Davis. The fort was just over the New Mexico border, and just north of the border to Old Mexico. According to the map the largest town near Fort Davis was Ciudad Juarez, in Mexico, and that was two hundred miles. He knew they would encounter some smaller towns along the way, but once he got paid and paid his men, he knew they would head for Juarez for some R & R. But that was a long way off.

Forty-five days off, to be exact.

Ethan was going to be learning along the way. He had been a soldier for many years. He had been a rancher for only two, and it was a business he was learning by doing. The same thing he was now doing with this drive.

So he watched Taggart and the other men who were more experienced, learned and passed the knowledge on to the rest of the crew. He figured it might take them all a week to get comfortable with this task—including himself.

* * *

THERE WERE NO problems by the end of the first day. It was fall, so it didn't appear that weather would pose any difficulty. Again, Ethan left it to his foreman, Taggart, to call it a day. He assigned the men their jobs of standing watch at night, to be sure none of the horses wandered off, or were stolen.

The men had switched mounts in and out of the remuda during the course of the day, and now they unsaddled their mounts and turned them over to the wrangler. The men going on watch would do so with fresh mounts.

The chuck wagon brought up the rear, it came driving into camp well after they had stopped. Moze and Abraham quickly got set up to cook for the men. The hands were also able to refill their canteens from barrels of water lashed to the outside of the wagon.

The two Black men decided that the easiest thing to cook and dish out on this first night would be chuck-wagon stew. They built a fire and got the huge pot going, and soon the smell had mouths watering.

"Come and get it!" Abraham shouted, and the men lined up. He and Moze gave each man an empty bowl and ladled out the stew for them.

"Here you go, boss," Moze said, handing Ethan a bowl of stew.

"Thanks, Moze," Ethan said, "but in the future I'll stand in line like everybody else."

"Sure, boss."

Taggart and Granger got their bowls and came over to eat with Ethan and discuss the day.

"How much ground you think we covered, George?" Ethan asked Taggart.

"We did okay, boss," Taggart said. "Probably about twenty-five miles or so."

"Then we're already behind," Ethan said. "We've gotta make at least thirty. We'll need to get an early start tomorrow, stop later, and drive 'em harder."

"We can drive till dusk, boss," Taggart said, "but we ain't goin' nowhere in the dark."

"I know that," Ethan said. "We're just gonna have to figure it out."

Granger ate quickly, which Ethan noticed.

"What's your hurry?" he asked.

"I'm gonna ride night watch with a couple of the boys who've done it before. I need to get my feet wet, Ethan. This has been an interestin' day, but I'm still anxious to learn more."

"That's good," Ethan said. "I should probably do the same thing, at some point."

Granger carried his empty bowl back to the wagon and handed it to Abraham, then went to get his horse. He wanted a mount beneath him that he was familiar with.

"It was our first day, Ethan," Taggart said. "Most of the men are doin' what Granger's doin', gettin' their feet wet. Hell, that's what you're doin'."

"I know," Ethan said, "but I want them to learn fast—and that goes for me, too."

"Don't worry," Taggart said, "we'll get the herd movin' faster."

"First day and I'm already a bundle of nerves," Ethan complained. "You got any whiskey?"

"You said no whiskey on the drive, remember?" Taggart reminded him.

"You took me seriously?"

"I sure did," Taggart said. "The last thing we need is some drunk cowboys, and that goes for you, too."

"Yeah, yeah," Ethan said. He had a small bottle of whiskey in his saddlebags, but there was no way he could let the men see him pulling from it, so it had to stay where it was.

Taggart finished his bowl and stood up.

"I'm gonna see if any of the men have any questions after today," he said.

"Good thinkin'," Ethan said. "That's why you're the foreman and I'm just the owner."

"It's our first night out, Ethan," Taggart said, "you should relax. Think things over. We still have lots of decisions to make."

"I know we do," Ethan said. "You're right. I'll see you later."

Taggart walked away and Ethan sat by the fire and finished his stew. Moze came over to get his bowl and spoon.

"Moze . . ."

"I know, boss," Moze said, "from now on you'll bring me the empty bowl. How about some coffee?"

"Sounds good."

"I'll bring it to you," Moze said, "just for tonight, okay?"

"Sure, Moze," Ethan said. "Make sure all the men get fed, will you?"

"Sure, boss."

Moze went back to the chuck wagon, and returned with a cup of strong black coffee.

"Thanks."

"Sure, boss. I'm gonna go help Abraham clean up now."

"Go ahead."

"You okay, boss?"

"I'm fine, Moze," Ethan said. "I'm gettin' adjusted, like everyone else."

Moze went back to the chuck wagon while Ethan drank his coffee. It was a quiet night, and he thought he could hear the herd moving around.

Most everyone had finished eating and some of them were turning in, some others were sitting up and talking. After two years they still treated Ethan like he was Captain Miller, which meant leaving him to himself, like in the war. The only thing was, in the war he always had his own tent. Now he was out in the open like the rest of them. He wondered if he should be mixing with his men, or maintaining his distance? After all, they always had to remember that he was the boss.

Soon they were all asleep, except for the ones on night watch. Ethan's eyes were drooping, so he unfurled his bedroll and made himself comfortable. He was asleep in minutes.

# CHAPTER THIRTEEN

IN THE MORNING Ethan woke to the smell of chuck-wagon breakfast hash. The men were already lined up, holding their plates.

"You're up."

He turned his head, saw Taggart sitting, eating.

"Moze and Abraham outdid themselves this morning," Taggart said. "You better go and get some before it's all gone."

"Right."

He stood up and went to get in line. The men in front of him offered to let him go first, but he told them he would wait his turn.

When he reached the front of the line Moze gave him a tin plate of hash, and a tin cup of coffee. He carried them back to where Taggart was sitting.

"How's the herd?" he asked.

"Fine," Taggart said.

Ethan looked around.

"Where's Grange?"

"Out with the herd."

"Did he sleep?"

"He did, then he got up, ate breakfast before anyone else, and went back out."

"He's gonna run himself ragged before we even get started," Ethan said. "Send somebody out to get 'im."

"Right."

While waiting for Granger, Ethan stomped out his fire, made sure his men did the same, then told them all to get saddled up. Moze and Abraham got busy packing up the chuck wagon.

Granger came riding in, and Ethan was surprised to see his friend look so fresh and awake.

"What are you doin'?" he asked.

"Just learnin', Ethan," Granger said, dismounting, "gettin' ready to do my part. This is gonna be a long trip."

"You can say that again," Ethan said, "and you're gonna wear yourself out."

"Nah, I'm fine," Granger said. "I'm really likin' this work."

"What's to like about it?" Ethan said. "It's gonna be backbreaking."

"Sitting out there on my horse on night watch?" Granger said. "It's so quiet."

"Just wait till we're out here a few weeks, then tell me how quiet and peaceful it is."

"I'm gonna get some water for my canteen," Grange said, and walked over to the chuck wagon.

Ethan went and saddled his own horse, mounted up and rode over to the buckboard.

"You fellas ready?" he asked Moze and Abraham.

"Yessuh," Moze said. "We's all ready."

Abraham nodded.

Taggart rode up next to Ethan.

"We're gonna start movin' the herd," he said.

"Okay," Ethan said, "I'll be right behind you. I'm gonna ride with Moze and Abraham for a while."

Ethan saw Granger ride out with the rest of the men. He had a big smile on his face. There was nothing about this drive that made Ethan want to smile.

When everyone was out of camp and riding the herd Moze picked up the reins of the chuck wagon. Abraham climbed up onto the seat next to him.

"Let's move out, Moze," Ethan said.

"Yessuh!"


WHEN ETHAN WASN'T riding the herd, he was riding alongside the chuck wagon. Normally, the man he would talk to most of the time was Granger, but his friend was totally absorbed with trying to become a trail hand. He had never been happy as a soldier, which was why he wanted to remain a sergeant and always turned down promotions. He just wanted to do his job. That was what he had been doing for the past two years. But this . . . this was totally new for him, new and freeing. He rode the herd during the day and rode the watch at night. When he was in camp he slept a few hours, and hardly talked with Ethan.

So Ethan started riding alongside the chuck wagon, talking with Moze and Abraham. He would have spoken with Taggart, but being the foreman he was busy doing his job. And since Ethan still had to keep his distance from his men as their boss, the only men he could talk to were the two Black cooks.


THE FIRST PROBLEM appeared at the two weeks' mark. They were actually still driving the herd through Wyoming, and had almost reached Cheyenne. After riding almost five hundred miles one of the men came riding up to Ethan. It was Stackhouse, the wrangler.

"You're supposed to be with the remuda," Ethan said.

"I know that, boss," Stackhouse said. "It's the chuck wagon. I looked back and didn't see it, so I rode back a ways and found them."

"Found them?"

"Yeah," Stackhouse said. "Somethin's wrong. It was either a wheel or an axle."

"Okay, Stack," Ethan said. "Go on back to the remuda. I'll take care of it."

"Yessir."

Stackhouse rode off and Ethan rode around the herd until he found Taggart.

"What's up, boss?" Taggart asked, as Ethan rode up alongside him.

"The chuck wagon," Ethan said. "There's a problem. A wheel or an axle. Who do we have that can fix somethin' like that?"

"That'd be Rex Winstead, he's our repair guy."

"Where is he?"

Taggart looked around.

"I'll find him and meet you at the chuck wagon," he said.

"Okay."

Ethan rode back, past Stackhouse and the remuda, kept going until he saw the chuck wagon. It was leaning to one side. Moze and Abraham were standing on the ground, looking at it.

"Are you all right?" Ethan asked.

"We fine, boss," Moze said.

"We cain't say de same for de wagon, boss," Abraham said.

"I can see that."

Ethan dismounted and walked around the wagon.

When he got to the other side he saw that one of the wheels had cracked. He knew it could be repaired, but that would take time. And hopefully there was no trouble with the axle.

He walked completely around the wagon and stopped when he came to Moze and Abraham again.

"Did we pack a spare wheel?" he asked.

"Yessuh," Abraham said. "I gots it in de back of de wagon."

"Well, I got help comin'," Ethan said. "Taggart and Rex Winstead. The five of us ought to be able to handle it, and the herd can keep movin'."

Moments later they heard two horses approaching and then Taggart and Winstead rode up.

"You keep the herd movin'?" Ethan asked Taggart.

"Yep," Taggart said. "I told Grange to keep take over and we'd catch up."

Winstead immediately walked to the wagon, and where Ethan had walked around it, he quickly crawled underneath it. After a few moments he reappeared, slapping his hands together.

"The wheel's gotta be replaced, but there's no problem with the axle."

"That's good," Ethan said. "There's another one in the back of the wagon."

"Then let's get it fixed. Once we stop for the night I can see about repairin' it."

Winstead and Abraham got the spare wheel out of the back of the wagon and got to work. As they looked on Taggart said to Ethan, "And just how are we gonna lift the wagon? There are no branches around that I can see."

"That's why there's a two-by-six piece of wood in the wagon, to use just for something like this."

"I keep forgettin' that you think of everythin'."

"Not everythin', but I try," Ethan said.

\* \* \*

AFTER MOZE AND Abraham unloaded some of the equipment from the wagon to lighten it, Ethan, Taggart, Moze, and Abraham lifted the wagon just high enough for Winstead to remove the damaged wheel and then slide the spare on. Then he greased the wheel and the axle. When they lowered the wagon to the ground, the new wheel held.

Moze and Abraham got back on the seat together, and Moze picked up the reins.

"You must've hit a pretty big rock," Winstead observed. "Keep a sharp eye out, because we ain't got another wheel—least 'ways not till I can repair the broke one."

"We'll be careful," Moze said.

"You boys ride on up ahead and catch up to the herd," Ethan said. "I'll ride with the chuck wagon for a while, just to make sure the wheel holds."

"Okay," Taggart said. He looked at Winstead. "Let's go."

The two of them rode off. Ethan mounted up and headed over to the wagon.

"Moze, go easy at first," Ethan said. "Once we know it's gonna hold you can speed up."

"Gotcha, boss."

Moze snapped the reins at the team and started forward. Ethan rode alongside.

JUST TO BE on the safe side, Ethan circled the wagon, keeping an eye on the new wheel. After about a half an hour he rode up alongside Moze.

"Okay, Moze," he said. "Let's speed it up."

"How far you t'ink we gone, Cap'n?" Moze asked.

"Ten days? Maybe three hundred miles," Ethan

said, guessing. Taggart was the one who would know. "If we're lucky, and we're on schedule."

"Come on, Cap'n," Moze said, with a smile. "We's always lucky."

B Y THE TIME they caught up to the herd they had made camp for the night.

"About time," Granger said, with a grin. "Everybody's starvin'."

"I gets the stew started," Moze promised.

"Stew again?" Granger asked.

"We ain't had stew since the first night, Mr. Granger," Abraham said.

"Is that right?" Granger asked. "Well, okay, then. Stew it is."

"Tell the men supper will be soon," Ethan told him, dismounting.

"Right," Granger said, reaching for the horse's reins. "I'll take him for you."

"Thanks," Ethan said. "I've gotta get cleaned up."

After washing up Ethan got in line for supper with the other men and waited patiently.

# CHAPTER FOURTEEN

IN CAMP THAT night Taggart said, "Three hundred miles is a good guess."

"Then we're makin' good time so far," Ethan said.

"Looks like it," Taggart said. "We're lucky the chuck wagon problem wasn't bigger. It didn't hold us up."

Ethan looked across the camp to where Rex Winstead was repairing the broken wheel.

Ethan and Taggart were eating chunky stew from a bowl. Winstead had a bowl near him, taking a bite every so often. The other men sitting around were eating, except for the ones on night watch.

"Where's Grange?" Ethan asked.

"Where do you think?"

"What's wrong with him?"

"He's discovered a whole new world," Taggart said. "And he likes it."

"I'm afraid he's not thinkin' straight."

"We've got another problem," Taggart said.

"What is it?"

"The man I sent ahead to scout—Stevens—came back. He says we've got Indian trouble up ahead."

"What kind of trouble, exactly?"

"He thinks Apache," Taggart said.

"How many?"

"A small party."

"War party?" Ethan asked.

"He thinks a huntin' party."

"How many?"

"Half a dozen, maybe," Taggart said.

"All right," Ethan said. "We'll be on the lookout. We might have to trade with them."

"Horses?"

"A few, and maybe some food. Tell Moze and Abraham to be ready."

"They'll get somethin' together," Taggart said.

"Pass the word," Ethan said. "Nobody fires a shot unless I do."

"Got it." Taggart stood up. "I'll pass the word."

Ethan nodded and kept eating while Taggart walked away. Then he stood and carried his bowl over to where Winstead was working.

"Why don't you take a break and eat," he suggested.

"I can do both, Cap'n," Winstead said.

"Will we be able to use this wheel again if we have to?" Ethan asked.

"If Moze doesn't try to go too fast, yes," Winstead said.

*Like if we have to run from Indians*, Ethan thought, but he said, "Let's hope that doesn't happen. When you're finished with that wheel, take the rest of the night off."

"No night watch on the herd?"

"No night watch."

Winstead looked up from his work.

"I appreciate that." He picked up his bowl, took a spoonful of stew, then set it down and went back to the wheel. Ethan carried his empty bowl over to the chuck wagon.

"Mo', suh?" Moze asked.

"Did all the men eat?"

"Not yet."

"Then I had enough," Ethan said. "Where's Abraham?"

"He's in the wagon, puttin' some food in a bag in case we run into Apaches."

"That's good. I'll take a cup of coffee, Moze."

"Yessuh."

He took the coffee to his fire, sat and lit one of the few cigars he had left. He had been rationing them out, one every night or two. At that rate he could last another week.

Taggart came walking over with a cup of coffee and sat across from him.

"All the men have been told about the Apaches," he said.

"You sendin' Stevens out to scout again tomorrow?" Ethan asked.

"Yeah, I am."

"Send another man with him," Ethan said. "Don't let him go alone."

"The Apaches are just as likely to attack two men as one," Taggart pointed out.

"Still, I'd feel better if he had somebody with him," Ethan said. "He can choose a man."

"I'll tell 'im."

"Well, look what the cat dragged in," Ethan said, looking past Taggart. The foreman turned and saw Granger riding in. He dismounted, handed his horse off to Stackhouse, then walked to the chuck wagon. He came walking over to Ethan and Taggart, carrying a cup of coffee.

"No food?" Ethan asked.

"I came in and ate earlier," Granger said, squatting down by the fire. Ethan was sitting on his saddle, while Taggart was on a thick branch.

"You gonna get some sleep?" Ethan asked.

"Right after I drink this coffee," Granger said. "What are you two talkin' about?"

"Apaches," Taggart said.

"I heard that from Bennett when he came out to relieve me," Granger said. "Are we worried?"

"We're preparin' ourselves," Ethan said.

"You give 'em some horses they'll probably leave us alone," Granger offered.

"Maybe," Ethan said. "We're also puttin' together some food offerings."

"That could work, too."

"They might want guns," Taggart said.

"We can't give the Apaches guns," Ethan said. "Let's understand that."

"We do," Granger said.

"Right," Taggart said. "No guns."

"Do we have anythin' else to worry about?" Ethan asked.

"Like what?" Granger asked.

"Rustlers?" Taggart asked, "Is that what you're thinkin'?"

"You can't drive two hundred head without bein' noticed," Ethan said. "Call Bennett over, will ya?"

"I'll get 'im," Taggart said.

He stood up and walked further into the camp to where a group of men were eating. When he came back he had Harve Bennett with him.

"What d'ya need, Cap'n?" Bennett asked.

"Did you see anythin' other than Apaches?" Ethan asked.

"Anythin', or anybody?" Bennett asked.

"Either," Ethan said. "Anythin' to make you think we were bein' watched by somebody other than Indians."

"I saw a man on a horse," Bennett said.

"A white man?"

"Yessir."

"What was he doin'?"

"Ridin'," Bennett said. "I thought he was runnin' from the Apaches. In fact, that's how I saw the Indians, but they didn't see me. Watchin' this guy ridin' warned me."

"Which way was he goin'?" Ethan asked. "He didn't come back this way."

"He was headin' west," Bennett said.

"If he's a man alone we got nothin' to worry about," Granger said.

"And if he's a scout for rustlers," Ethan said, "we gotta keep our eyes peeled west, just in case."

"I can do that, Cap'n," Bennett said, "and I'll be takin' Ben Treadway with me."

Ethan knew both Bennett and Treadway were good men.

"We'll head out early tomorrow mornin'," Bennett said.

"Okay," Ethan said, "but stay alert and if anythin' happens, don't be heroes. Just hightail it back to us. Whatever it is, we'll handle it together."

"Yes, sir."

Bennett went back to the other men.

"We better all get some sleep," Taggart said.

"Set a watch," Ethan said. "I don't want anybody, red or white, comin' up on us by surprise."

"Right, boss," Taggart said.

The foreman went to see about setting the watches.

"I'm turnin' in," Granger said, standing up. "Listen, I know I've been actin' strange."

"You have?" Ethan asked, smiling.

"Startin' tomorrow, boss, you tell me what you want me to do, and I'll do it."

"I'm gonna hold you to that, Grange," Ethan said. "G'night."

"Night."

Ethan spread his bedroll out and lay down on his back, staring at the sky. He didn't know if they'd have to deal with Apaches tomorrow, or something else, but he did know they had to be ready for anything.

E THAN WOKE IN time to see Bennett and Treadway ride out of camp. Taggart saw him getting to his feet and walked over.

"Time for breakfast," the foreman said.

They headed over to the chuck wagon and stood in line. It was a cool morning, so Moze and Abraham had prepared some hot cornmeal mush and hotcakes. That and coffee would warm everyone's belly. Later in the day, when the sun was high, the temperatures would rise.

Taggart and Ethan took their bowls and cups over to Ethan's bedroll, and were soon joined by Granger.

"Startin' today we're gonna be pushin' even harder," Ethan said. "We're gonna go slightly to the east so we can pass by Colorado Springs. We can't be takin' this herd through the mountains."

"Once we get into the flats of New Mexico," Taggart said, "we should be able to move even faster."

"And by then," Ethan said, "we'll have some idea of whether or not we're gonna make the deadline."

"Colorado Springs is about two hundred miles from

here," Granger observed. "And that should be the half-way point."

"Good," Ethan said. "We'll know more when we get there."

"And we'll probably need some supplies by then," Taggart said.

"We'll worry about that later," Ethan said. "Let's break camp and get this herd goin'."

B ENNETT AND TREADWAY rode from morning till afternoon without seeing anybody.

"Where did you see the Apaches?" Treadway asked.

"A little farther ahead," Bennett said. "But this is about where I saw the lone rider. I'm sure he must've been runnin' from those Indians."

"But you didn't see any of them chasin' him?" Treadway asked.

"Maybe they're stayin' put, waitin' for us," Bennett said.

"If they know we're comin'," Treadway said, "then they must've sent back a scout."

"Yeah," Bennett said, "let's look out for one lone Apache rider."

"Right."

They topped a rise just ahead of them, reined in, and turned their horses when they saw the Apache on the other side.

"Damn!" Treadway said. "Think they saw us?"

"If they did, they'd be ridin' already," Bennett said. "Ben, you gotta go back and warn the cap'n. Tell him to swing the herd east or west of here. Maybe we can avoid runnin' into the redskins."

"We're supposed to stay together," Treadway said.

"The boss has gotta be warned."

"Then let's go and warn him together."

"Naw," Bennett said, "one of us has to keep eyes on these Apaches. You go, I'll be fine."

"Bennett, if they see you," Treadway said, "you run like hell."

"You can bet on it," Bennett said.

# CHAPTER FIFTEEN

BENNETT KEPT WATCH on the Indian camp. The herd was safe as long as these braves were still in place. Once they moved, all bets would be off.

But it didn't look like they were moving anytime soon. There were more than half a dozen tepees set up, with women and children moving around. But he didn't see many men, which probably meant the hunting party was still out.

He decided he had better return to the herd and tell Ethan Miller that the hunting party was out there, now that he knew a little more than Treadway did. Avoiding this camp would only keep them from interacting with women and children. That wasn't worth adding extra time to the drive.

He backed away from the rise, mounted his horse, and started off in Treadway's wake. He probably wouldn't beat him back to the herd, but he could keep them from acting on Treadway's information, which was incomplete.

Bennett figured he was halfway back to the herd when he saw Treadway's horse ahead of him. It was just standing there. As he got closer he saw a body lying on the ground. It had to be Treadway.

When he reached the body he reined in and dismounted. Turning the body over, he saw the arrow in Treadway's chest. They had shot him out of his saddle, and he had fallen onto the ground face first, driving the arrow in deeper, while breaking part of it off.

He looked around quickly to see if he was being watched. Seeing no one, he crouched over Treadway to check him, hoping he was still alive. But the man was dead. Half of the shaft was sticking out of his chest; the other half was on the ground next to him.

Hurriedly, Bennett lifted Treadway's body onto his horse and tied it there. Then he picked up the other half of the arrow and put it in his saddlebag. After that, he mounted and, leading Treadway's horse, headed out.

WHEN HE GOT to the herd several of the hands came riding out to meet him. One of the riders was Granger.

"What the hell happened?" Granger asked.

"We split up," Bennett said. "Treadway was comin' back here, but I found him later with an arrow in his chest."

"We better get to the cap'n and let him know," Granger said. "The rest of you stay with the herd."

The others nodded and rode back.

"Where's the cap'n?" Bennett asked.

"He went to check on the progress of the chuck wagon," Granger said. "We can meet up with him there."

They headed back toward the tail of the herd, where they found the chuck wagon following behind, Ethan riding alongside, talking with Moze and Abraham. As they approached, both Ethan and the chuck wagon stopped.

"Bennett," Ethan called, "what happened?"

"I'm sorry, sir," Bennett said. "We split up and the Apaches killed him. He's got an arrow in his chest. Well, half an arrow." Bennett reached into his saddlebags. "Here's the other half."

Ethan took the arrow from Bennett.

"Grange, you notice anythin' about this arrow?" Ethan asked.

Granger reached out and took the shaft.

"Yeah, this ain't an Apache arrow. It's Arapahoe." He handed it back to Ethan. "But the Arapahoe are about to sign a treaty. It's been three years since the whole Sand Creek Massacre thing."

The Sand Creek Massacre in Southern Colorado Territory occurred when a group of ranchers accused the Arapahoe of violent attacks, bringing the Third Colorado Cavalry into the mix. After as many as five hundred Arapahoe were massacred—including women and children—it turned out the ranchers were lying, because they hated Indians. Since that time, there had been trouble between the Arapahoe and the whites, but recently there was talk of a treaty.

"There are always those who don't want to give up on a war," Ethan said. "Even now there are Southerners who haven't admitted the South lost the war. In this case, I can't say I blame the Arapahoe."

"Hopefully," Granger said, "this is just a small huntin' party."

"There *are* Apaches out there, though," Bennett said. "We're gonna hafta watch for both of them."

"Agreed," Ethan said. "But first we're gonna bury Treadway."

"What about the herd?" Granger asked.

"We'll let it keep goin'," Ethan said, "and catch up afterward."

"But the men," Granger said, "they'd probably wanna, you know, pay their respects."

"I'm sorry about that," Ethan said, "but we can't stop the herd, Grange. Not with that deadline. Hopefully, the men will understand."

"They might," Granger said, "if you're the one who explains it to them."

"Who else?" Ethan asked.


B ENNETT AND GRANGER buried Treadway's body. Ethan said a few words over the grave, while Moze and Abraham hummed a hymn. The five men all made a contribution to the man's interment.

"Let's get movin'," Ethan said, afterward. "We'll catch up to the herd after they've stopped to camp."

"They're gonna wonder where we are," Granger said.

"That's why you and Bennett will ride ahead and join them. I'll come along later with the chuck wagon. By then I'll know what I want to say to them."

"So you don't want us to say nothin'," Granger said.

"No," Ethan said, "we already decided that'd be my job."

"You want me to scout up ahead again, boss?" Bennett asked.

"No," Ethan said, "I want you to stay with the herd. I don't wanna come across your body with an arrow in it."

Bennett seemed relieved. He and Granger mounted up and rode on ahead at a gallop.

"You wants us to push, boss?" Moze asked.

"No," Ethan said, "I don't wanna lose another wheel."

"The mens gon' be hungry," Abraham said.

"We'll catch up and you fellas can make somethin' extra good for the men. That stew you make is perfect."

"Sure, boss," Abraham said, "I makes de stew."

"Then let's get goin'," Ethan said. "And I want you each to keep an eye out from your side of the wagon."

"Yes, boss," Moze said.

Moze and Abraham climbed aboard the chuck wagon; Ethan mounted up and they started off.

B OSS?" MOZE SAID.
    "I see them."

After about an hour they saw the braves off to their right, keeping pace while riding a ridge. There seemed to be half a dozen of them.

"Dem's 'rapahoes?" Abraham asked.

"I can't tell from here," Ethan said. "They might be Apaches or Cheyenne."

"Are dey at war, too?" Moze asked.

"The Cheyenne and the Arapahoe were affected by the Sand Creek Massacre," Ethan said. "I never heard anythin' about Apaches bein' there."

"Why dey jus' followin' us?" Moze asked.

"I don't know," Ethan said. "The easiest answer is, they wanna see where we're goin'."

"So what we do?" Moze asked.

"We let 'em follow," Ethan said. "There's not much else we can do."

"What if deys come down after us?" Abraham asked.

"Just keep your guns handy," Ethan said, "but don't fire unless I do."

"Yessuh, Cap'n," Moze said.

T HEY CAUGHT UP to the herd as dusk came. The men had made camp, built campfires, picketed the remuda, and assigned night guards on the herd.

"Thank God," Taggart said, as the chuck wagon pulled into camp. "The men are starvin'."

"We's get de stew goin'," Abraham promised, as he and Moze climbed down.

"Grange told me what happened," Taggart said.

"Did you tell the men about Treadway?" Ethan asked.

"No."

"That's good. I'll tell 'em, but we have other problems."

"Like?" Taggart asked.

"We were followed all the way here," Ethan said.

"Arapahoe?"

"I couldn't tell," Ethan said. "Could be Cheyenne, or Apaches. They were too far away, but close enough to watch us and keep track."

Taggart looked out into the darkness.

"So they could be out there right now," he said.

"Right."

"How many?"

"Six, that I saw," Ethan said.

"Cap'n, we gotta tell everybody."

"And we will," Ethan said. "Call 'em all in, but leave two men on the herd. Tell them what's goin' on, and that they'll have help, and be relieved so they can eat."

"Yeah, okay," Taggart said.

Ethan nodded, looked around as Taggart went off to gather the men, and saw Granger. He walked over to his friend, who knew more about Indians than he did.

He told Granger about the Indians who followed them, described them as best he could.

"They sound like Apaches to me," Granger said.

"Will they come at us at night?" Ethan asked.

"It's not true that Indians don't attack at night,"

Granger said, "but it also depends on the tribes and their habits and customs. There's six of them, you said?"

"That's right."

"Why would they attack at night?" Granger asked. "They can see they're outnumbered. Why didn't they attack you when it was just you, Moze, and Abraham?"

"Maybe they're waitin' for help," Ethan said.

"If they've been watchin' us, it's been longer than just today," Granger said. "I think they're gonna approach us in the next few days—maybe even tomorrow. They'll probably wanna trade."

"That's if they're Apaches," Ethan said.

"Right," Granger said. "If they're Arapahoe or Cheyenne, we could be in trouble. They might very well be watchin' us, waitin' for more of their brothers to arrive."

"So what can we do?"

"We keep watchin', and we keep movin'," Granger said. "They know we've seen 'em, so we got to act like we ain't concerned, at all."

"But we are," Ethan said.

"Well, we know that," Granger said. "We jus' don't want them to know it."

# CHAPTER SIXTEEN

A LL THE MEN got fed and filled in on Treadway's
death, on the Arapahoe and the Apaches. They
weren't happy about Treadway being buried out on the
prairie somewhere without them being able to pay
their last respects, but for the most part they understood.

They did, however, sit around the fire and tell stories about their friend's exploits, before, during, and
after the war. There were happy and sad moments.

Four men were left on the herd for each watch, then
relieved so they could come in and eat. From the time
they stopped and camped until morning Ethan wanted
three shifts of four men each, three hours at a time. He
didn't want anybody falling asleep in the saddle.

He sat and ate his stew with Taggart and Granger.

"You wanna break out that bottle of whiskey?"
Granger asked Ethan.

"What bottle of whiskey?" Taggart asked, looking
at Ethan.

"The one you have hidden in your saddlebags," Granger said to Ethan. "The one I know you brought along in case of emergency, and haven't cracked yet."

"Oh," Ethan said, "that bottle. I thought about it, but I don't need a bunch of hungover cowboys in the mornin'. I think the boys are doin' just fine without it."

"Trading with some Apaches ain't gonna hold us up much," Granger said, changing the subject, "but if they're Arapahoe, and they attack—"

"I know," Ethan said.

"—the deadline'll be the least of our worries," Granger finished.

"I know," Ethan said, again.

"Then we just have to hope they're Apaches," Taggart said, "don't we?"

"Maybe," Granger said, "we should make the first move."

"How?" Ethan asked.

"If we see 'em watchin' us in the mornin'," Taggart suggested, "we should mount up, you and me, and ride toward them, see what they do."

"They might open fire," Granger said.

"Or they might turn and run," Taggart said, "in which case we'd know we don't have to worry about them."

"And if they stand their ground," Ethan said, "we trade with them."

"Right," Taggart said.

Ethan looked at Granger.

"What d'ya think, Grange?"

"It's gotta be better than just waitin' for 'em to make a move," he said. "Only I think it should be you and me, Ethan."

"Why?" Taggart asked.

"You're the foreman, George," Granger said. "If somethin' goes wrong, we need you to be in charge."

"Okay, then," Ethan said. "Let's turn in and get an early start. If we can trade with them and get it done, we won't lose any time. In fact, George, when me and Grange ride out to them, you can start the herd movin'."

"Gotcha, boss," Taggart said.

Ethan walked to the chuck wagon to talk with Moze and Abraham.

"I want a good breakfast in the mornin'," he told them. "I want it to keep them goin' all day long."

"Yessuh, boss," Abraham said. "I's do sausages, sweet taters and biscuits."

"Sounds good, Abe," Ethan said.

With breakfast and the day's activities set, Ethan settled down into his bedroll. But despite what Granger had said about the Apaches attacking at night, he didn't sleep very well . . .


IN THE MORNING the Apaches were in plain sight, looking down on the camp and the herd from atop a hill. It made the men restless. Even during the hot breakfast some of them would touch their guns, as if to make sure they were still there and ready.

"I've got an idea," Granger said.

"What's that?" Ethan asked.

"I don't know how the men would feel about it, but it might get us some information about the Arapahoe."

"Go ahead."

"Let's invite them to breakfast."

Ethan looked out at the six Apaches.

"The Apaches?" he said.

"They're probably hungry," Granger said. "We give them a hot breakfast, some extra food and few horses . . . and we ask them what they know about the Arapahoe."

Ethan thought a moment, then said, "We'll have to

let the men know what we're doin' so nobody's surprised."

"Right."

Most of the hands were having breakfast, except for the ones who were still riding the herd.

"All right," Ethan said, "I'll tell the men here in camp. Taggart can go out and inform the men who are on the herd. Then you and me, we'll go out and extend the invitation.

WHEN ALL THE men had been informed, Ethan and Granger saddled their horses, mounted up, and rode out to where the Apaches were sitting on their ponies. The six men just sat and waited.

Ethan and Granger reined their horses in, and for a few moments they and the Apaches just stared at each other. All six braves were large strapping young men. Granger knew a little of the Apache language, but Ethan wanted to try English first.

"Do any of you speak English?" he asked.

"I speak white man's tongue," one of the braves said.

"My name is Ethan," Ethan said. "This is Granger."

"I am Stands Tall Man."

From what Ethan could figure, examining all the six men, Stands Tall Man seemed to be the shortest, but he figured, what the hell.

"We would like to invite you to eat with us," Ethan said. "We have hot food ready."

Stands Tall Man turned to his braves and said something, to which they all nodded.

"We come," he said to Ethan.

"Good," Ethan said, "follow us, then."

Ethan and Granger led the six braves into camp. The men stood back and gave them room to dismount

and approach the chuck wagon. The braves stared at
Moze and Abraham, and then one of them ran his fin-
ger over Moze's face and then showed his fingertips to
his brothers. Apparently, they had never seen a Black
man before.

"I will have someone see to your ponies," Ethan
said to Stands Tall Man.

The brave hesitated, then grunted and nodded.

Moze and Abraham made sure each brave got a
bowl filled with sausages, sweet taters, and biscuits.
Luckily, it was all food they could eat with their hands.
They ate gingerly until they got used to the heat, and
then scarfed the food down.

Ethan and Granger ate their breakfast with the
Apaches. The rest of the men had already eaten, so
they just stood back and watched. Four of them
mounted up and rode out to spell the others on the
herd, so they could come in and eat. When the new
men arrived they stared at the Apaches warily, got
their food and walked off to the side to eat.

When the Indians had all emptied their bowls, they
held them out to Moze for more. Luckily, Abraham
had made plenty. Once again the Apaches attacked the
food with gusto, washing it down with cups of water
Moze supplied.

"No whiskey?" one brave asked, at one point.

Ethan looked at Stands Tall Man and said, "Sorry,
we don't have any whiskey."

The braves nodded and went back to eating.

After breakfast Abraham carried a gunnysack
filled with food over to Stands Tall Man and handed it
to him. He grunted and accepted.

"Why have you been watchin' us?" Ethan finally
asked.

"You have many fine horses," Stands Tall Man said.

"I do," Ethan said. "I'm taking them to Texas to sell."

"Apaches need horses," Stands Tall Man said.

"I'll tell you what," Ethan said "I'll give each of your braves a horse if you'll answer some questions for us."

"What questions?" Stands Tall Man asked.

"About the Arapahoe," Ethan said. "They have killed one of my men. I want to know how many of them there are, and if we're gonna have to fight them."

Stands Tall Man thought about that for a moment, then held up two fingers.

"Two horses for each brave," he said.

"One horse for each brave," Ethan countered, "but two for Stands Tall Man."

Stands Tall Man thought about that for a few moments, then nodded.

"Grange," Ethan said, "why don't you talk with our friend and see how much you can find out. I'll arrange for the horses to be culled from the herd."

"Okay, boss."

Ethan left Granger squatting at a fire with the Apaches. He sent two men out to the herd and told them to come back with seven good horses.

"Any seven, Cap'n?" one of the men asked.

Ethan looked back at Stands Tall Man for a moment, then said, "Make as many of them as you can paints."

"Right."

The two men mounted their horses and rode out. They returned fairly quickly with seven horses, five of which were paints, and two roans. Ethan had bridles and reins put on them. Even though the Apaches didn't use saddles and bridles, he figured they'd need the reins to lead the animals away.

Ethan walked to where Granger, Stands Tall Man, and the other braves were all standing up.

"Your horses are ready," Ethan said to Stands Tall Man.

Then he waved and two men brought over the seven horses, as well as the ponies the braves had ridden in on. "They're not broke," Ethan said. "You'll have to do that yourself."

Stands Tall Man nodded. He and his men mounted their ponies, grabbed the reins of the horses they would be leading, and then rode out of camp.

"Not even a thank-you?" one of the men said, as the Apaches left.

"Apaches don't say thank you," Granger said.

The two men who had fetched the horses shrugged, turned, and walked away.

Tensions within the camp faded away the further the Apaches got.

"Let's get the herd movin'!" Taggart shouted.

While the foreman and the hands all mounted up and rode out to the herd, and the two Black men packed the chuck wagon, Ethan stood off to one side with Granger so no one would overhear their conversation.

"What did you get from them?" Ethan asked.

"The Arapahoe that killed Treadway are a hunting party of about eight," Granger said. "Stands Tall Man doesn't think they'll attack. There are too many of us."

"Will they want to trade?" Ethan asked.

"The Arapahoe are not looking to trade with the white man," Granger said. "If they don't figure they can kill us, they'll leave us alone."

"What do you think of all that?"

"Stands Tall Man seems to know what he's talkin' about," Granger said.

"Is he a chief?" Ethan asked.

"No, but he wants to be," Granger said. "Right now he just leads those boys who were with 'im."

"So they won't be watchin' us anymore?" Ethan asked.

"They might," Granger said, "but that would just be to make sure the Arapahoe don't attack."

"They're gonna protect us?"

"They appreciated the food and the horses," Granger said. "They don't want anythin' to happen to us."

"Okay, then," Ethan said, "it sounds like we all want the same thing."

"You were smart to give Stands Tall Man two horses," Granger said. "It showed respect."

"I make a right decision every once in a while," Ethan pointed out.

# CHAPTER SEVENTEEN

STANDS TALL MAN and his braves accompanied
Ethan and his herd until they were out of Colorado
Territory. As the herd bypassed the town of Trinidad
and crossed into New Mexico Territory, Stands Tall
Man raised his right hand in farewell. Ethan waved
back, turned to Granger and Taggart.

"That's it," he said. "No more Apaches or Arapahoe."

"Not exactly true," Granger said. "There are Jaca-
rilla Indians in New Mexico, and they're technically
Apaches. We'll also have to watch out for Kiowa, Na-
vajo, Pueblo, even some Comanches—"

"Okay, I get it," Ethan said. "We'll be on the lookout at all times."

"We've got about twenty days to do another five
hundred miles," Taggart said. "We don't need any Indian trouble."

"No, we don't," Ethan said. "We'll have to send
scouts ahead of us again."

"Not Bennett," Taggart said. "He's been through enough."

"Agreed," Ethan said. "You and Grange pick out two men. Make sure they don't split up."

"Right," Taggart said.

"And let's keep this herd movin'."

THE FIRST NIGHT they camped in New Mexico Territory Ethan had to admit he kind of missed their Apache chaperone.

"More coffee, Cap'n?" Moze asked, standing over Ethan with the pot.

"Moze—"

"I was bringin' Mr. Granger some more, thought I'd stop by you, also, suh," Moze said, quickly.

Ethan turned and looked at Granger, who lifted his coffee cup to him.

"Yes, I'll have some more," Ethan said to Moze. "Thanks."

"Suh," Moze said, and filled his cup.

Granger came walking over and squatted down by the fire with Ethan.

"You're deep in thought," he observed. "We're gonna make the deadline. We've been movin' at a good pace."

"I know it," Ethan said.

"Then what's on your mind?" Granger asked.

"Indians."

"What about them?"

"Worrying about Indians has kept my mind off other possibilities."

"You mean like rustlers?"

"I still can't help thinkin' that the army might try somethin' to make us miss the deadline."

"Like sending rustlers after us?" Granger asked. "You really think the military might hire rustlers?"

"I'm thinkin' about the military *bein'* the rustlers," Ethan said.

"And you figure they'd go so far as to put some soldiers in trail duds and order them to stop us?" Granger asked. "You think they'd get enough soldiers to follow an order like that?"

"There were soldiers who did some pretty awful things durin' the war because they were under orders," Ethan reminded him.

"Ethan," Granger said, "I think we've got enough to worry about with Indians. But if the military is gonna try somethin' to make us miss the deadline at Fort Davis, I think they'd do it close to Fort Davis."

"When they know we're gonna make the deadline," Ethan said. "Which means they'd have to have us watched."

"What are you two talkin' about?" Taggart asked, coming over to join them.

"Ethan's tryin' to give himself more to worry about," Granger said.

"Like what?"

"Like cavalrymen dressed as rustlers."

"Hell," Taggart said, "I wouldn't put that past the army."

"Jesus," Granger said, "you two are bein' . . . what's that word?"

"Overly distrustful?" Ethan asked.

"That's it," Granger said, pointing at him. "Distrustful."

"Maybe so," Taggart said, "but there's no harm in keepin' a sharp eye out."

"Who did you two agree to send out as scouts?"

"We only had to agree on one, Cap'n," Taggart said.

"Bennett insisted he wanted to go out. We're sending Johnny Wyatt out with 'im."

"Good men," Ethan said. "Just tell 'em to watch out for more than just Indians."

"Will do," Taggart said. "You know what I could use right now?"

"A cold beer," Granger said.

"Exactly!"

Ethan thought about the bottle of whiskey in his saddlebag. He left it there. If he didn't follow the rules he himself laid down he couldn't expect anybody else to.

THE NEXT MORNING Travis and Wyatt went out, with strict instructions to stay together. If they had some sort of news to report, they were to return to the herd together.

Ethan watched them ride off, hoping they would return healthy and with some kind of good news . . .

LIEUTENANT COLONEL WESLEY Merritt, the commanding officer of Fort Davis, looked up from his desk when there was a knock at his door.

"Come!" he shouted.

The door opened and his adjutant, Lieutenant Jess Foley stuck his head in.

"Colonel, Sergeant Jackson is here to see you?"

"Jackson?" Merritt frowned. "Who's he?"

"You know, sir, he's one of the, uh, Buffalo Soldiers."

"Buffalo sold—oh, you mean the negroes?"

"Yes, sir."

"Send him in."

The door opened and a large Black man entered, his shoulders and arms straining the seams of his uniform, the sergeant's stripes on his sleeve shining very white.

"Colonel," he said, saluting.

Merritt returned the salute in a very relaxed manner.

"What can I do for you, Sergeant?"

"Sir, the men of the Ninth are itching to perform some sort of service, sir. We didn't sign up just to sit around and look good in our uniforms."

Merritt gaped at the big negro.

"Where the hell did you learn to talk?"

"I went to college in Philadelphia, sir," Sergeant Ezekial Jackson said. "I signed up when the war broke out."

"As a private?"

"Yes, sir.

"So you've worked your way up to sergeant?"

"Yes, sir," Jackson said. "I like to think it was because I do my duty, which is all my men want to do."

"What is it you'd like to do, Sergeant?"

"Fight, sir," Jackson said. "We're here to fight. Since we got here two months ago all we've been doing is manual labor, laying railroad tracks, which is something a Chinaman can do."

"Who's been givin' you your orders, Sergeant?"

"Captain Windham, sir."

"Then why aren't you talkin' to him about this?"

"I did, sir," Jackson said.

"And what did he say?"

"Sir," Jackson answered, "he said niggers were supposed to do what they're told without question."

Merritt frowned.

"You were never a slave, were you, Jackson?"

"No, sir," Jackson said, "I've been a free man all my life."

"And the other men of the Ninth?"

"Some were free, some are freed slaves," Jackson said.

"All right, Sergeant," Merritt said, "I'll talk to Windham, and see if we can't come up with something your Ninth can do."

"Thank you, sir."

"When you leave, send my adjutant in, will you?"

"Yessir."

"Dismissed."

The big negro left the office, and Lieutenant Foley rushed in.

"Yes, sir?"

"Tell me about Captain Franklin Windham, Foley," Merritt said. "Did he fight in the war?"

"Yes, sir, he did."

"Which side?"

"I believe he was a Confederate soldier, sir."

"What rank?"

"I believe when the war ended he was a colonel."

Ah . . . that would probably explain his attitude toward the Buffalo Soldiers, Merritt thought.

"Tell him I want to see him," Merritt said.

"Yes, sir," Foley said, "right away."

"And Foley."

"Yes, sir?"

"How many days do we have left in that deadline for the horses arriving from Montana Territory?"

"About three weeks, sir."

Merritt gave the young lieutenant a hard look.

"I don't want to hear 'about,' Lieutenant."

"I'm sorry, sir," Foley said. "There are nineteen days left."

"Let me know when there's a week left," Merritt told his adjutant. "I'll want to send out scouts."

"Yes, sir, I'll do that, sir."

"Dismissed."

Foley saluted and left.

Merritt turned and looked at the map on the wall behind him. The six hundred miles that stretched between the Rio Grande and Concho Rivers were lined with forts. Troops A, B, C, and K were commanded by Colonel Hatch at Fort Stockton. Merritt commanded Troops D, F, G, H, and I at Fort Davis. And now the Ninth Cavalry Buffalo Soldiers had been added to his command.

There were six forts—including Stockton, Lancaster, Davis, Duncan, McKavett, and Concho—between Forts Quitman and Clark. They were all tasked with trying to keep settlers safe from the Apaches, Kiowa, and Comanches who lived in the region. To do that he was going to need weapons and horses. He was waiting for deliveries of each, the horses from the north, and the weapons from the east.

The horses were coming as the result of a civilian purchase, while the weapons were being shipped by the army. The weapons were due within the next two weeks and now he knew the horses were coming in the next nineteen days or so. The civilian they were purchased from was one Ethan Miller, who had been a captain in the Union Army during the war.

Merritt was familiar with Miller's name and background. The man had been something of a hero, but had chosen to muster out rather than accept a promotion. Merritt knew the army didn't like that, and his orders were to accept delivery of the horses, and pay Miller what was owed, according to his contract. If he made his deadline. And Merritt had been told, in no uncertain terms, that the army would not be upset if Miller missed his deadline.

Merritt did not like being told to sabotage the delivery of the horses. He had a lot of respect for Ethan

Miller, although the two men had ever met. The man had walked away from the army and made a life for himself. What right did the army have to interfere with it?

Another knock on his door broke into his reverie. He turned from the map and said, "Come!"

Foley stuck his head in and said, "Captain Windham is here, sir."

"Send him in."

Windham entered, his hat beneath his left arm, and saluted with his right hand. He was tall, with slate-gray hair and eyebrows and a firm-set jaw. A contemporary of Merritt's, Windham was the kind of man who should have been more than a captain by now, if not for the fact that he had served the Confederacy during the war. When Confederate officers joined the US Army, they were usually reduced in rank.

"You asked to see me, suh?" he asked, in his Southern drawl.

"Captain," Merritt said, "what's this I hear about you referring to our Buffalo Soldiers as niggers?"

Captain Windham stared at Colonel Merritt as if he didn't understand the question.

"Isn't that what they are, sir?" he asked.

# CHAPTER EIGHTEEN

THEY GOT THE herd halfway through New Mexico Territory without any problems.

"The way we're movin'," Granger said, as they ate their supper, "we'll be passin' just east of El Paso."

"At that point we'll turn the herd east and head for Fort Davis."

"What if we delivered the horses to Fort Stockton, or Quitman?" Taggart asked. "Wouldn't that help us make the deadline?"

"I don't want the army to have any reason to say we didn't fulfill our contract," Ethan said. "We agreed to deliver to Fort Davis."

"Besides," Granger added, "it looks like we're gonna make the delivery date."

So far Bennett and Wyatt had returned each night reporting no sign of Indians or rustlers.

"You know as we get closer to Fort Davis we're gonna see Kiowa, and probably Comanches," Granger said. "That'll be our last challenge."

"Seein' 'em ain't the problem," Taggart said. "It's dealin' with 'em. It won't be as easy as it was with Stands Tall Man and his Apaches."

"We've got two weeks left," Ethan said. "There's a lot that can happen in two weeks."

"Or nothin' can happen," Granger said.

"Yeah, what are the chances of that?" Taggart asked.

Ethan felt the same way. So far the only obstruction they'd had was the Apaches, which they'd handled just right. And they had lost only one man, Treadway, to an Arapahoe arrow. But after that, no one had even gotten sick or injured along the way. They hadn't lost one man or one horse, which was unusual. They were down only the seven head they had given to the Apaches. Ethan wondered how long this good run of luck could last.

"You're still lookin' for trouble," Granger said to him.

"Better to look for it and not find it, than the other way around," Ethan said.

"You got that right," Taggart said.

"Cap'n?"

They all looked up at the man who had approached them.

"What is it . . . Cunningham?"

"Weatherly ain't feelin' too good, sir," Cunningham said. "He's been pukin' since we made camp."

Ethan looked at Granger while Taggart stood up and said, "I'll have a look, boss." He followed Cunningham.

"I know what you're thinkin'," Granger said. "It's probably somethin' he ate didn't agree with 'im."

"If there was somethin' wrong with the food, there'd be others pukin'," Ethan pointed out.

"There's nothin' wrong with the food," Granger said. "Moze and Abraham know what they're doin'; they keep things clean, and they don't let nothing go to waste, or go bad."

"Well," Ethan said, getting to his feet, "let's find out what's goin' on."

Granger stood up and followed Ethan.

They crossed the camp and found Taggart and Cunningham leaning over another man who was heaving, but who had nothing left to heave.

"What's wrong with 'im?" Ethan asked.

"Dunno, boss," Taggart said, "'cept he can't seem to keep anythin' down."

"Get Moze over here," Ethan said. In the absence of a doctor, they usually left it to Moze to treat the sick or injured. So far there had been a few injured who Moze had patched up, but this was the first sick man.

Taggart sent Cunningham to fetch Moze.

As Moze came rushing up and bent over Weatherly, Ethan, Granger, and Taggart backed away a few steps. Some of the other men gathered around to watch.

"Is he okay, boss?" Bennett asked Ethan.

"That's what we're tryin' to find out, Bennett," Ethan said.

"If he's sick—" Bennett started.

"Let's just wait and see what Moze has to say," Ethan suggested.

Bennett nodded and faded back to join the other men who were gathered.

"Whatcha got, Moze?" Ethan asked.

"I ain't sure, boss," Moze said. "His stomach ain't holdin' nothin' down, but nobody else has the same trouble. I got a tonic I gon' give 'im to see if it settles 'im."

As Moze returned to the chuck wagon for the tonic, Ethan walked over to Weatherly.

"How you doin', Weatherly?" he said.

"N-not so good, sir," Weatherly said, still bent over. "I don't think I can ride herd tonight."

"Don't worry about that, son," Ethan said. "Moze is gonna give you somethin' to help ya."

Weatherly nodded, clutching his stomach.

Granger came up behind Ethan.

"You think he just doesn't wanna ride night herd?" Granger asked.

"He's pretty pale," Ethan said. "I don't think he's fakin'."

Moze returned with his tonic and had Weatherly drink some of it, then stretch out on his bedroll.

Ethan pulled Moze aside.

"Does he have a fever?"

"No, suh."

"So you don't think he's got somethin' he's gonna spread to the men?"

"No, suh."

"Then what is it?" Ethan said.

"Could jes' be a upset stomach, suh," Moze said. "If dat be's it, den my tonic and a good night's sleep gon' fix 'im."

"I hope so," Ethan said.

"I's keep my eye on him, suh," Moze said.

"Thanks, Moze."

Ethan went back to his fire to sit with Granger and Taggart. The other men sat at the various fires in camp. Ethan hoped they would get through the night without anyone else falling sick.

"I'm turnin' in," Taggart said.

"I'll take the first watch," Granger said. "I ain't that tired."

"That's because you stopped ridin' the herd every night," Ethan said.

"It was relaxin' for a while," Granger said, "but I got bored with it."

"Well, don't stay up on watch too late," Ethan said. "I'm, gonna need you at your best for the next two weeks or so."

"I gotcha, boss," Granger said.

"I'll take a watch tomorrow night," Ethan promised.

"Hey," Granger said, "you're the boss, remember?"

"Still," Ethan said, "I gotta do my part."

Ethan bedded down, but now he not only worried about the possibility of Indians or rustlers, but disease, as well . . .

W HEN ETHAN WOKE the next morning the first thing he wanted was a report on Weatherly's condition. He got to his feet and looked around for Moze. He found him with Abraham, at the chuck wagon.

"How did Weatherly make it through the night?" he asked.

"Pretty good, Cap'n," Moze said. "He woke up this mornin' sayin' he was hungry. We gave him some breakfast, an' he kept it down."

"Looks like your tonic did the trick," Ethan said.

"Yessuh," Moze said.

"You wants yo breakfast, since you're here, suh?" Abraham asked.

"No," Ethan said, "let the men line up. I'll come back when they've all been fed."

"Yessuh," Abraham said.

"Thanks, Moze."

Moze nodded, and went back to helping Abraham get the breakfast ready.

Bennett and Wyatt got in line first, so they'd be able to ride out early. The rest of the men lined up behind them.

"Goin' last again?" Granger asked, coming up alongside Ethan.

"Yep."

"How'd Weatherly get through the night?"

"Accordin' to Moze he slept fine and woke up hungry."

"So was he fakin', or did Moze's tonic do the trick?" Granger asked.

"I'd say it was either the tonic," Ethan said, "or whatever made him feel sick didn't last long. Anybody else sick?"

"Nope, nobody," Granger said. "They're all either lined up for breakfast, or out with the herd."

"Where's Taggart?"

"He's with the herd, makin' sure it's ready to move as soon as breakfast is finished."

"What about supplies?" Ethan asked.

They had made a couple of supply runs to small towns along the way, nothing two men wouldn't have been able to handle.

"We're good," Granger said. "Might need some food before we get to Fort Davis, but we'll see." He shrugged. "Maybe we can pick up some game."

"Sounds good."

As they ate their breakfast—bacon and johnnycakes today—Taggart came riding in. He left his horse saddled, approached a group of men and touched one on the shoulder. The man nodded, drained his cup, and went to get his horse. Taggart spoke to the other men, who also nodded. Then he got in line for food. Carrying his plate and cup to where Granger and Ethan were sitting, he announced, "Weatherly got through the night," he said, as he sat with them.

By this time the man he had picked had ridden out to the herd.

"So we heard," Ethan said. "Hopefully it was nothin' but an upset stomach. Nothin' he can pass along to any of the other men."

Granger looked over at the chuck wagon, saw that everyone had been fed.

"You want more?" he asked Ethan. "I'm gonna see if they've got more."

"Sure, if they have it," Ethan said, handing his plate and empty cup over.

"How's the herd?" he asked Taggart. "Any trouble?"

"No more than usual," Taggart said. "We had a few head stray durin' the night, but at first light we found 'em and drove them back into the herd."

Four other men finished their breakfasts, mounted up, and rode to the herd to spell the men there, so they could also eat before they got the herd moving.

"You've got these men runnin' like a fine-tuned clock," Ethan said to Taggart.

"They're good boys, Ethan," Taggart said. "You wouldn't have brought them with you to Paradise if they weren't."

"That's true."

Four men rode in and hurried to the chuck wagon for their breakfasts. After that they'd have to exchange their horses for fresh ones from the remuda.

"What are we gonna do after we deliver the herd?" Taggart asked.

Granger returned at that moment with two plates, handed Ethan one. Behind him came Moze, carrying two steaming cups of coffee.

"Thanks, Moze," Ethan said. "You and Abraham eat, and then pack up."

"Yessuh."

"Talk about good boys," Taggart said, "those two run a tight chuck wagon."

"Yeah, they do," Ethan said. "What'd you ask me, George?"

"After we get paid," Taggart said, "what are we gonna do?"

"Head back," Ethan said.

"What about the men?" Taggart asked. "Are you gonna give them time to unwind?"

"Let me put it this way," Ethan said. "I'll be headin'

back. Anybody wants to come with me, can. Anybody who wants to unwind and come back later, that's okay, too."

"We're gonna be passin' near to El Paso," Taggart said. "I'm just thinkin' some of the boys might wanna stop there and have a little fun, after all their hard work."

"That'll be okay with me," Ethan said. "And either of you who needs to unwind. No problem."

"Why are you lookin' at me, Ethan?" Granger asked.

"Because you're the type who likes to unwind, Grange," Ethan said. "You'll probably set the tone for everyone else in El Paso."

"Well, if ya wanna unwind, El Paso's the place to do it," Granger said.

"You can do it without me, then," Ethan said. "I'll just wanna get back to Paradise."

"Let's just get through this last part of the trip," Granger said, "and then we can all get to enjoy the good parts."

They finished their breakfasts, broke camp, and got the herd headed out.

# CHAPTER NINETEEN

THE LAST WEEK of the drive turned out to be the hardest.

Once they bypassed El Paso and turned the herd east toward Fort Davis, the luck seemed to turn bad. A sandstorm one day held them up for hours, and after it passed they had to ride down horses who had strayed from the herd in their panic. They recovered them, but lost a few who had injured themselves and had to be put down.

On another day one of the hands, Travis, was riding down some strays, and his horse stepped into a chuck-hole. He was thrown, came down on his leg, which snapped in two. Taggart and some others had to quickly bind the leg to staunch the bleeding, as the bone had come right through the skin. They hurried him back to camp, where Moze worked on him, setting the leg, bandaging it and, hopefully, saving it.

Ethan watched the activities closely, then said to

Moze and Abraham, "Make room for Travis in your wagon. He'll be ridin' the rest of the way with you."

"Yes, boss," Abraham said.

And at the end of that last week, as they thought they would have no trouble making Fort Davis in time, Bennett and Wyatt came riding back with a vengeance.

"What's wrong?" Ethan asked, as they reached him in a heavy cloud of dust.

"Comanches, boss!" Bennett said.

"How many?" Ethan asked.

"A lot!" Wyatt said.

"I counted twenty-five, boss," Bennett said. "Maybe more."

"Can we avoid them?" Taggart asked. "Go around them?"

"*We* could go around them," Bennett said, "but not with the herd."

"Well, we ain't leavin' them the herd," Ethan said, "so we're gonna hafta fight 'em." He looked at Taggart. "Get the rifles out of the chuck wagon. Take two men with you to help arm everyone."

"Right."

As Taggart rode back to the chuck wagon with two men, Granger moved his horse closer to Ethan's. They both looked out over the sea of horseflesh they had driven fourteen hundred miles.

"We ain't gonna be able to fight 'em off," Granger said. "Not if there's twenty-five, or more."

"We can fight 'em," Ethan said.

"Not without losing most of the herd," Granger said. "We either have to lose the herd, or the men, Ethan."

"You're sayin' run, and leave the herd?" Ethan asked.

"The men will choose to stay and fight with you," Granger said, "and die. You'll have to order them to run."

"We came all this way . . ." Ethan said, shaking his head.

"I know," Granger said. "It's a hard decision."

Ethan looked at Bennett.

"How long have we got?" he asked.

"They weren't movin'," Bennett said. "They're waitin'."

"We've got some time," Granger said. "If you order the men to run, it'll be a while before the Comanches decide to ride. When they realize the herd is theirs, they won't hunt the men."

"Gather everybody," Ethan said.

Granger nodded, gave Bennett and Wyatt orders.


TAGGART AND HIS two men were going to ride out to the herd with rifles and arm everyone. He was surprised to see all the men riding to the wagon, following Ethan.

"What's goin' on?" Taggart asked.

"Hold off on the rifles for a bit," Ethan said. "I wanna talk to the men."

Taggart waved his two men away from the wagon. The others gathered around on their horses. Ethan remained mounted as he turned to face his hands.

He explained the situation. They were facing a superior number of Comanches. It appeared they could save themselves, or try to save the herd and suffer heavy loses.

"Or we could all get killed and they'll take the horses, anyway," he finished. "It's been suggested to me that I order all of you to run."

"Just like that, Cap'n?" somebody asked. "We didn't run during the war when we was outnumbered."

A few men nodded their agreement to that.

"We drove this herd too far to let it go," another man added.

That brought more nods.

"Okay, then," Ethan said. "If we stay and fight, I won't hold it against any man who wants to leave."

"A lot of us *wanna* leave, Cap'n," Bennett said. "But we won't."

"All right, then," Ethan said to Taggart, "hand out the rifles. Bennett, come with me."

Ethan and Bennett rode off to one side.

"You said we could go around them," Ethan said. "You could do that alone, couldn't you?"

"Yessir, no problem."

"Then you ride," Ethan said. "Get to Fort Davis and bring back help. We'll hold 'em off for as long as we can."

"You're gonna need cover, boss," Bennett said, "and it's flat between here and them."

"No cover?"

Bennett thought a moment.

"There was somethin'," Bennett said. "Looked like it used to be a church. It's rubble now, but there might be enough of the walls left to use as cover."

"Well," Ethan said, "that'd be better than shootin' some of the herd and building a wall of horses to hide behind. Where is this church?"

"Wyatt can take you," Bennett said. "He's the one who spotted it."

"Okay," Ethan said, "get Stack to give you a fresh horse, and go."

"Yessir."

Ethan rode back to where the men were being given rifles. He pulled Wyatt aside.

"Sure, I know where that church is," the young man said.

"Okay," Ethan said, "wait here."

Ethan rode and brought Granger and Taggart back with him. He went over the plan again.

"What do we do with the herd while we're hidin' in a church?" Granger asked.

"We take 'em with us," Ethan said. "Drive 'em close to the church, but not so close that the shootin' will spook 'em."

"Why not spook 'em on purpose?" Granger said. "Stampede them right at the Comanches?"

"That's gonna be a last resort," Ethan said. "Even if we do that and come out of it alive, it would take us forever to gather them up, again."

"So you wanna try and fight off the Comanches," Taggart said, "but keep the herd together. How do we do that?"

"With Treadway gone, and Bennett ridin' for the fort, there's fifteen of us left. Moze and Abraham can handle rifles. We take cover at this church, and leave three men with the herd to keep them from spookin'. And if we end up needin' a stampede, they can do it."

"What if the Comanches don't come after us?" Granger asked. "What if they go for the herd?"

"Then the three men run," Ethan said. "I don't expect them to stand there and be slaughtered."

Ethan could see that both Granger and Taggart were thinking. They were all destined to be slaughtered.

"Look," he said, "we don't have to beat 'em, we just have to hold 'em off until the cavalry gets here."

"If Bennett gets through," Granger said.

"He'll get through," Ethan said "We just don't know if they'll get here in time."

WELL-ARMED, THE MEN rode back to the herd, and then followed Wyatt as he led them to the fallen church. Wyatt stopped short, at one point, and Ethan rode up and joined him.

"Where is it?"

"'bout a mile ahead."

"I can't see it."

"It's all stone," Wyatt said. "it blends in."

"Why stop here, then?"

"Sir, I didn't know how close you wanted to take the herd," Wyatt said.

"That's good thinkin', son," Ethan said. He turned and waved to Granger and Taggart to join him.

"We'll leave the herd here," he said.

"Where's the church?" Granger asked.

"Up ahead," Ethan said. "Once we get there we'll be between the Comanches and the herd."

"And what if they go around us?" Taggart asked.

Ethan looked at Granger.

"You know Indians better than the rest of us," Ethan said. "Would they go around us and take the herd, or would they want to kill us, first?"

"The Comanches are warriors," Granger said, "not sneak thieves. They'll wanna go through us, not around."

"Can we count on that?" Taggart asked.

"No," Granger said, frankly.

"Ain't the Kiowa and Comanches supposed to be on reservations?" Taggart asked.

"It looks like these don't wanna go," Granger said. He looked at Wyatt. "You notice how they were armed?"

"Bows and arrows," Wyatt said. "No guns."

"Thank the Lord for small favors," Granger said to Ethan.

"George, pick out three men to stay with the herd," Ethan said. "Then we'll ride."

IT DIDN'T TAKE long to cover the mile to the church.

"Wow," Granger said, when they reached it, "there ain't much left in the way of walls."

"It'll do," Ethan said.

"We only knew it was a church because the bell tower is left," Wyatt said, pointing.

"That's good," Ethan said to Taggart. "Put two men in that tower. They'll be able to warn us when the Comanches are comin', and they'll get good shots off from there."

Granger stared at the bell tower for a few moments, then said, "I wonder how many of us could get up there?"

# CHAPTER TWENTY

Ethan spread the men out to find cover behind whatever was left of the church walls. The highest sections they could find were about three feet tall. Others were two or one. Some of the men had to lie on their bellies with the barrels of their rifles resting on top of the one-foot walls.

"They're comin'!" Wyatt suddenly shouted from the bell tower. "And there's more than we thought."

Ethan walked over to the base of the tower and looked up.

"How many?"

"Boss, could be fifty or more," Wyatt said.

*Damn*, Ethan thought.

"Can you see the herd from your vantage point?"

Wyatt went to the other side of the tower.

"Yes, sir," he said. "They look like they're standin' calm."

Ethan just hoped the three men he had left with the herd could keep them calm when the shooting started.

He wasn't sure exactly how much farther they had to go to get to Fort Davis, but however long it would have taken them with the herd, Bennett could make it faster on his own. He hoped his man would be able to convince the CO to send help.

"Still comin', boss," Wyatt called down.

Ethan went and joined his men who were stationed behind the three-foot wall.

"Nobody fires until I do!" he called out.

They all agreed, and since he had fought with these men in the war, he knew none of them would panic and fire first.

While they were outnumbered, the only advantage they had was superior fire power. But while Ethan was well experienced fighting another army, he knew nothing about fighting Indians.

"Grange," he said to his friend, who was next to him, "are we gonna be able to discourage them so that they'll quit after the first charge?"

"No," Granger said. "They're used to ridin' into rifle fire. It doesn't scare them. When they turn back, it's only to regroup and come again, and again, and again, until they overrun their enemy."

"Great," Ethan said, "thanks."

"Like you said," Granger reminded him, "we just have to discourage them long enough for Bennett to get here with help."

"If the fort wants these horses," Ethan said, "it shouldn't be too hard for Bennett to convince them."

"Depending on what kind of an ass the CO is," Granger said. He never had a high opinion of officers, which was the main reason he don't want to be one.

"They stopped!" Wyatt called.

Ethan stood and stared into the distance.

"I can see them," he said.

Granger stood.

"They're spreadin' out," he said. "They wanna show us how many of them there are, to scare us."

"They're doin' a good job," Ethan said. "Looks like Wyatt's last count might be right—fifty or more."

"They're gonna make us wait," Granger said.

"Till when?" Taggart asked, from Ethan's other side.

"Till they're ready," Granger said, "but they'll come well before dark."

"That gives them a lot of hours to work with," Ethan observed. "But the longer they wait, the better chance we have of gettin' help from the fort."

Granger started to say something, then stopped.

"What?" Ethan said.

"I was just gonna say . . . if Bennett got through."

That statement was followed by silence.


"THEY'RE MOVIN'!" WYATT shouted.

On the ground they could hear the sound of horses as the Comanches got closer, and then the war cries of the braves.

"Yeah," Granger said, "this time they're comin' in."

"Everybody get ready!" Ethan shouted.

There was the sound of metal on metal as weapons were readied. Then, from a cloud of dust, the Comanches were there, arrows flying.

"Fire!" Ethan shouted.

The first volley of shots took Comanches from their horses, but that didn't stop the others from coming. Ethan and his men worked the levers on their rifles as quickly as they could. As the attacking Indians got closer some of the men, who were more comfortable with them, pulled their pistols and brought them into play.

And just when Ethan thought the Comanches would keep coming and overrun them, they turned and headed back the way they had come. Some were injured and on foot, others lying face up or face down, dead.

It was over.

"That was the first wave!" Granger called out. "Get reloaded."

"Anybody hurt?" Ethan asked, looking around.

Heads turned as everyone surveyed the area. It seemed every man on the ground was okay.

"Wyatt! You two all right up there?" Ethan called.

"Yes, sir, we're fine," Wyatt said. The other man waved.

"What are they doin'?" Ethan asked.

"Regroupin'," Wyatt told him.

"They'll be back," Granger said, standing next to Ethan and reloading his rifle and pistol. "They'll just make us wait a while."

Ethan looked at the ground around them littered with arrows. Some were simply scattered about, others were buried point first in the dirt. The first group were fired straight on, while the others were lofted at an angle, in an attempt to injure or kill the men as they took cover behind the remaining walls.

"They'll adjust their attack," Granger said. "We should move our people around."

"What do you suggest, Grange?"

"I think they'll center their attack on this three-foot wall, where most of us were shooting from. Let's spread out."

Ethan looked at what was left of the other walls.

"Let's put some men at the base of the bell tower," he said. "That'll be adequate cover from the arrows, no matter what angle they loose them from."

"Good thinkin', boss," Granger said. "Once they realize we've put men there, where their arrows can't do any harm, they'll withdraw again to refigure their attack."

"And the third time they come?" Ethan asked.

"They'll overrun us," Granger predicted. "Then we'll be hand-to-hand and outnumbered."

Ethan turned and started giving orders. He also called for the chuck wagon to be used as extra cover.

HARVE BENNETT MADE it to Fort Davis without encountering the Comanches. Since he was a single rider, they opened the gates for him. From there he convinced the officer of the day to let him see the commanding officer.

Lieutenant Colonel Wesley Merritt looked up from his desk as his adjutant brought the man in.

"You wanted to see me?" he asked.

"My name's Bennett. I'm ridin' with Ethan Miller, to deliver his horses to the fort."

"Are you here to tell me he's not going to make tomorrow's deadline?"

"No, sir," Bennett said, "I'm, here to tell you he's pinned down by Comanches, and if you want your horses, you're gonna have to get 'im out."

"Foley!" Merritt shouted.

"Yes, sir?" his adjutant said, poking his head in.

"Get me my officers, on the double."

"Yessir!"

As Foley withdrew, Merritt asked Bennett, "Where are they?"

"I ain't sure," Bennett said, "but it used to be a church. Now it's just . . . rubble. But Captain Miller is using it for cover."

"And where's the herd?"

"About a mile behind that," Bennett said.

"So Miller and his men are between the Comanches and the herd?"

"Yessir."

Merritt stood up and turned to his map.

"That's got to be the Santo Domingo Church," he said. "It's been wasting away for years." He turned to look at Bennett. "Is there really enough of it left for adequate cover?"

"For a while, sir," Bennett said. "But I don't know how long the captain and his men will be able to hold it."

"Captain?"

"I served with him in the war, sir," Bennett said. "We all did."

"So he has experienced fighting men," Merritt said.

"Oh, yessir!" Bennett said.

"Then maybe he can hold his position and give us a chance to get there," Merritt said. "It must have taken you two hours to ride out here."

"Yessir, I guess. Probably more because I had to avoid the Comanches."

"We can have the post doctor look you over, get you some clean clothes—"

"If you don't mind, sir," Bennett said, "I just need some water and a fresh horse."

"All right," Merritt said.

Foley knocked and stuck his head in.

"Your officers are here, sir."

"Send them in," Merritt said. "And Foley, see that this man has water and a fresh horse."

"Yessir!"

Half a dozen officers entered the CO's office and he immediately outlined the problem to them. Bennett stood aside and listened.

"Now get your men mounted," Merritt ordered. "Three troops should do it. We don't want a blood-bath, we just want to chase them off."

"Yessir," most of the officers said, and hurried out. One man remained behind.

"Sir, if I may speak?"

Bennett noticed the captain had a Southern accent.

"What is it, Captain?"

"The Comanches won't attack at night, sir," Windham said. "If we wait till mornin' to ride out there, the deadline won't be met, and the herd will be ours."

"You sonofa—" Bennett started, but Merritt waved him off.

"Captain, I'm not about to let a brave man and his crew die just to save the army some money."

"Sir, I only meant—"

"I know what you meant, Captain," Merritt said. "Your troop will not be going out there."

"Sir!"

"Dismissed!"

"Yessir."

As Windham left, Bennett said to Merritt, "He sounds like a grayback."

"He was," Merritt said. "You better get out there so my adjutant can get you situated."

"Yessir," Bennett said. "Thank you, sir."

# CHAPTER TWENTY-ONE

ALL THE MEN had a drink of water from the chuck wagon, and then hurried to their positions. Moze and Abraham took cover in the wagon with the injured man, Travis. Several of the men took cover behind or under the wagon. The three-foot wall that many had taken cover behind had been abandoned.

"Are you thinkin' about a stampede?" Granger asked Ethan.

"Goddammit, yes," Ethan said.

"If we survive this third wave," Granger said, "that might be the logical next step. When they come a fourth time I don't think they'll stop. They'll ride right over us."

"We could put more men in the bell tower," Ethan suggested.

"I know there's no bell, anymore," Granger said, "but there's still probably only room for two."

"We can't run," Ethan said. "That last charge scattered our mounts."

Granger looked at the sky.

"We're gettin' near to dusk," he said. "If they don't get us this time they might wait till mornin' to try again."

"They'd give us that much time to come up with a plan?" Ethan asked.

"No," Granger said, "they'd give us that much time to wait, worry, and be scared."

"Hey, boss!" Wyatt shouted from the bell tower.

"Yeah?"

"I see dust," he said, "lots of it."

"Where?"

"In the distance," Wyatt said. "Comin' up behind the Comanches."

"More Comanches?" Ethan asked.

"I can't tell," Wyatt said.

"All right," Ethan said, "keep a sharp eye out." He looked at Granger. "If it's more Indians, we're really done."

"Maybe it's Bennett and the cavalry."

"That's what we have to hope," Ethan said.

"They're comin' again!" Wyatt shouted.

"Make every shot count!" Ethan called out. "If we can hold them off this time they might leave us alone till mornin'."

"You heard the boss!" Taggart said. "Don't waste a shot!"

They could hear the horses coming, and all the rifles went up on the walls.

"How we doin' on ammo?" Granger wondered.

"Not a good time to ask, Grange," Ethan said. "Not a good time to ask."

IN THE BELL tower Wyatt squinted into the distance, trying to make out who was causing that big dust cloud.

"Can you make 'em out, Carl?" he asked Carl Denbow, the man he was sharing the tower with.

Denbow came to Wyatt's side of the tower and stared into the distance.

"Comanches," he said, "and a lot of dust comin' up behind them." He looked at Wyatt. "Could be Kiowa, comin' to help them."

"Or the army, comin' to help us," Wyatt said.

"If they leave us on our own," Denbow said, "we don't make the deadline, and we get killed. The army gets the herd."

"You think they'd let us all die for that?"

"You were in the war as long as I was," Denbow said to the younger Wyatt. "The army's got no shame."

"Jesus," Wyatt said, staring into the distance, "that's a big cloud." Then he noticed the Comanches moving again. "They're comin' again!" he shouted.


O N THE GROUND Taggart stared into the distance, but there was just enough of a rise that he couldn't see the Comanches from there.

"Come on," he said, "you three go behind the bell tower. The rest of you get behind those walls, or under the chuck wagon."

"That three-foot wall offers the most cover, boss," one man said.

"And that's where they'll expect us to be, James," Taggart said. "Just do what you're told."

"Yessir."

Taggart looked over to where Ethan and Granger were standing together. He might be the foreman, but he knew those two were friends. Ethan would always take Granger's advice over Taggart's. It was something the foreman had come to live with over the past two years.

"Boss?"

He turned and saw one of his men staring at him.

"What?"

"Where are you gonna be?"

"Oh, behind that two-foot wall," Taggart said. "I'd rather be on my knees than on my belly when they come."

"They're comin' again!" Wyatt shouted from the tower.

"Get to your station," he instructed the man.

"Right, boss."

Taggart looked out and saw the Comanches coming over that slight rise, into view. Good Lord, he thought, there seems to be more of them each time . . .

MOZE LOOKED OUT the front of the wagon, while Abraham was at the rear, with his rifle. Travis found a position in the center, where there was a hole in the side he could use as a gun port.

"I could use somethin' to eat right about now," Travis said.

"Dere's some dried beef dere," Abraham said, pointing, "and biscuits dere."

Travis looked at the meat and biscuits, and then said, "I could probably use a drink more."

"De boss say no whiskey on de drive," Abraham said.

"Yeah, but you guys've got some, don't ya?" Travis asked. "I could use it for the pain in my leg."

"Dem Comanches take you scalp," Moze said, "and you won' hafta worry 'bout yo leg." He and Abraham smiled at each other.

Then they heard Wyatt shout, "They're comin' again!"

*　*　*

"WE SHOULD'VE PRESET a signal from Wyatt to the herd," Granger said. "Just in case we wanted a stampede."

"He can see them," Ethan said, "but they can't see him."

"We coulda figured somethin' out."

"Like a torch?" Ethan asked.

"Maybe."

"Too late now," Ethan said. "We're in this till the end."

As the sound of the Indian ponies came closer, Granger said, "It won't be long, now."

"You know what we need?" Ethan asked his friend, as they both stared out into the dusty distance.

"A cannon?"

"Exactly."

"You're kiddin'."

"Well, we don't have one this time," Ethan said, "but let's look into gettin' one for the next drive. We can attach it to the rear of the chuck wagon."

"Are you serious?"

Ethan looked at Granger.

"I'm just makin' conversation till our guests get here," he said.

"Boss!" Wyatt shouted. "Cap'n."

"What?"

Wyatt pointed out toward the Comanches.

"Cavalry!"

When the men heard that they stood and cheered, but it was premature. Because they were standing, two men took arrows to the chest.

"Get down!" Ethan shouted. "And fire!"

They obeyed and started firing. But Ethan soon heard shots coming from behind the Comanches, as well as the sound of a bugle.

\* \* \*

THE COMANCHES BECAME aware of shots being fired from behind, and when they heard the bugle call they did not hesitate. Some veered around to face the oncoming soldiers.

Ethan stood immediately as a sea of blue came into view. As he watched the cavalry opened fire. Not just for effect, but with deadly accuracy. Blood flew as Comanches were shot from their horses. They sent arrows hurtling toward the soldiers, but without much effect. There weren't enough of them to make a dent, and they were certainly "outgunned," since all they had were bows and arrows.

As dead horses and Indians dotted the plains, the Comanches finally decided to fight another day. What was left of them veered left and right, and they ran.


DID WE LOSE anyone?" Ethan called out.

"Two," Taggart said, "Ellison and Ward."

"They shouldn't have stood up, damn it!" Ethan snapped.

As the soldiers advanced, Ethan stepped out into the open. He saw Bennett riding with them.

When they reined in Ethan smiled. "It's good to see you, Bennett."

"I brought some guests, sir," Bennett said. "Three troops of 'em. That's Captain Akers, leading A troop; Captain Palmer, B troop; and Captain Belford, C troop."

"We're happy to see you all," Ethan said.

Captain Akers, the older of the three, turned and yelled, "A troop, ride out and make sure the Comanches aren't regrouping. But don't pursue, and don't engage."

"Yes, sir," a sergeant said, and led A troop away.

Akers dismounted and approached Ethan.

"Captain Miller," he greeted, with a salute. "Did you lose anyone?"

"Two men," Ethan said. "Thanks to you, that's all."

"We've been ordered to secure you, your men, and your herd. We'll safeguard you all until we can get to the fort."

"I sure don't have a problem with that, Captain," Ethan said. "Our herd is about a mile out. We're gonna bring it up, and then deliver in the mornin'. Meanwhile, I think my cook can accommodate your men with a meal."

"Sounds good," Akers said. "The grub at the fort is . . . well, army grub."

Ethan turned and shouted toward the chuck wagon, "Moze, Abraham, get the fire goin'. We got guests for supper."

"Yessuh!" Moze called back. "Right away."

"This is as good a place as any for us to bivouac," Akers said.

"I don't think you'll need any tents for one night, do you, Captain?" Ethan asked.

Akers smiled.

"Probably not. We can sleep under the stars, and I'll post a watch in case those Indians decide to come back." He saluted again. "Excuse me."

He walked back to troops B and C, spoke with Captains Palmer and Bedford, and then started shouting at the men to dismount and make camp.

Ethan walked over to where Granger, Taggart, and others were slapping Bennett on the back.

"No trouble convincin' the CO to send us help, I see," he said.

"The army wants those horses, sir," Bennett said. "The colonel was happy to do it."

"Colonel?"

"Lieutenant Colonel Merritt, sir," Bennett said. "I never heard of him before, but he acted quickly."

"I never heard of him, either," Ethan said. He turned to Taggart. "Send some men for the herd, tell them to just drive them closer to us."

"Yessir."

The last men to arrive to pound on Bennett's back were Wyatt and Denbow, who had come down from the tower.

"You were a sight for sore eyes, buddy," Wyatt said, with a smile.

"Yeah," Denbow said, "you and a hundred soldiers."

"A hundred?" Granger said to Ethan. "We got enough food to feed 'em all?"

"It's our last night," Ethan said. "Moze and Abraham can empty our stores."

# CHAPTER TWENTY-TWO

With the number of men who were camped at Santo Domingo Church there were many campfires. And they anxiously lined up at the chuck wagon for Moze and Abraham to fill their plates.

"Wow, this is good grub," one soldier was heard to say.

"That's because you're used to army food," another said.

"Well then, I'm forgettin' the army and I'm gonna become a ranch hand."

Ethan sat off to one side and ate with Taggart, Granger, and Captain Akers.

"Looks like you're going to make your deadline, Captain Miller," Akers said.

"You don't have to call me captain," Ethan said. "Those days are gone. And yeah, I'm gonna make it, thanks to you and your men."

"You'll pardon me, sir, but I've heard of your exploits

during the war. I'd like to treat you with the respect you deserve."

"I appreciate that, Captain," Ethan said, "but a lot of my success came because of my men."

"Don't listen to him, Captain," Granger said. "He told us what to do, and we did it. It was all him."

"I guess that's the sign of a good commander," Akers said. "I wish my men were that loyal."

Ethan saw Bennett eating alone, sitting on the ground with his back to the three-foot wall.

"Excuse me," he said.

He walked over with his plate and hunkered down next to Bennett.

"You saved us, Bennett," Ethan said.

"I was lucky to get through, Cap'n, and lucky the post CO took me seriously."

"So, no problems?" Ethan asked.

"No problems," Bennett said, "but . . ."

"But what?"

Bennett looked around, like he wanted to make sure no one was close enough to hear.

"The CO, Colonel Merritt, called all his captains in and laid out the problem. One of them—a grayback— suggested they wait till mornin' to help us, so that we wouldn't make our deadline."

"A grayback in the army?" Ethan said. "The CO wouldn't go for that, huh?"

"No sir. He said he wasn't about to sacrifice lives to save the army some money."

"I'll look forward to meeting Colonel Merritt," Ethan said, "and that grayback. What was his name?"

"Lemme think," Bennett said. "Windham, I think."

"Franklin Windham?" Ethan asked.

"I think that was it," Bennett said. "You know 'im, Cap'n?"

"If it's the man I'm thinkin' of," Ethan said, "he was a colonel during the war."

"Then he must not be real happy he's a captain, these days," Bennett said.

"I'll bet."

"He's not gonna be a problem as long as Colonel Merritt's in charge," Bennett said. "After Windham made that suggestion, Merritt wouldn't let him ride out here."

Ethan looked back over at Captain Akers, who was now standing with his fellow officers.

"Lemme see what else I can find out," Ethan said, and walked over to join them.

"Ah, Captain Miller," Akers said. "This is Captain Palmer and Captain Belford."

"I should thank you gents for comin' to our rescue," Ethan said.

"It was our pleasure, Captain," Palmer said. He looked to still be on the light side of forty. Belford seemed a few years older.

"We all know of your reputation from the war, Captain," Belford said. "We're happy to keep you and your men alive."

"Accordin' to my men," Ethan said, "there was one captain at the fort who would've been just as happy to leave us till mornin'."

"Ah, you're talking about Captain Windham," Akers said.

"If he's the same man I'm thinkin' about," Ethan said, "he was a colonel in the Confederacy."

"That's him," Palmer said. "Grayback to the core."

"That makes it even funnier with Colonel Merritt putting Windham in charge of the Buffalo Soldiers," Akers said.

"Buffalo Soldiers?"

"A company of Blacks," Akers said. "Once they formed the Black regiments back in sixty-six to help fight the Indians, it was the redskins who dubbed them 'buffalo soldiers.'" The name stuck, and now all the Black regiments fall under that title."

"We had some back during the war," Ethan said. "How many regiments of them are there, now?"

"The Ninth and Tenth in the cavalry," Palmer said.

"Twenty-fourth and Twenty-fifth in the infantry," Belford added.

"We got the Ninth at Fort Davis," Akers said.

"And Windham's in command?" Ethan asked, shaking his head.

"Not if he keeps referring to them as 'niggers,'" Palmer said. "Colonel Merritt doesn't like it."

"I'll bet they don't either," Ethan said.

"That's only slightly better than when he calls the men 'Boy,' and expects them to kowtow to him."

"He must be chafin' under that blue uniform," Ethan said.

Belford laughed. "It's killin' him."

Moze came walking over to them, carrying a pot.

"If you fellas wants some more, this is the end of it," he said.

They all held out their plates.

"We'll get you restocked at the fort for your trip home," Akers assured Moze.

"I thank ya kindly, Cap'n," Moze said.

"He serve with you, too?" Palmer asked, as Moze went back to the chuck wagon.

"He did," Ethan said, "and Abraham's his cousin."

"Must have a lot of respect for you to follow you out West," Belford said.

"That works both ways," Ethan said. "You fellas enjoy your food. I'll see ya in the mornin'."

"You get a good night's rest, Captain," Akers said "We'll set a watch so you have nothing to worry about."

"Much obliged, Captain," Ethan said. "Much obliged."

IN THE MORNING all they had in the chuck wagon was coffee. Moze and Abraham filled everybody's cup, and then packed up the wagon.

"You need us to do anything, Captain?" Akers asked Ethan as his men rode out to the herd.

"Just accompany us to the fort, Captain," Ethan said. "Keep the Comanches off our backs, and make sure we get there."

"We can do that, Captain," Akers said. "We can surely do that."

Captain Akers got his men mounted and sent out scouts to make sure the Comanches were still scattered. With the rest of his troop, as well as B and C troops, he escorted Ethan and the herd to Fort Davis . . .

AFTER SEVERAL HOURS the herd was just outside the gates of Fort Davis. Captain Akers rode up to Ethan.

"My men will show your men where to put the horses," he said. "Meanwhile, the colonel would like to see you in his office."

"To get paid," Ethan said. "Lead the way, Captain."

Ethan turned and waved to Taggart and Grangers.

"The captain's men will show you where to put the horses," he said. "After that I'll meet you in the nearest saloon."

"We'll get them settled, boss," Taggart said.

"See you later," Granger said.

Ethan turned to face Akers.

"Let's go."

\* \* \*

WHEN THEY ARRIVED the colonel's adjutant, Lieutenant Foley, told them, "The colonel will be with you momentarily." He looked . . . agitated.

"What's going on, Lieutenant?" Captain Akers asked.

Nervously, Foley said, "I'm not supposed to—"

"Lieutenant!"

Foley looked around, then said, "We got word that the weapons we were expecting have . . . vanished."

"Vanished?" Akers asked. "You mean . . . been stolen?"

"We don't know," Foley said. "They were shipped from the East and they're not here."

"So they're somewhere in between," Akers said.

"Theoretically, yes," Foley said.

"Excuse me," Ethan said, "but this has nothin' to do with me. I'd like to see the colonel and be paid."

"Yessir," Foley said. "It'll be a matter of moments, sir."

Abruptly, the door to the colonel's office slammed open and a gray-haired officer wearing captain's bars came storming out. Then he turned and shouted into the office, "If you think I'm goin' out there with only a bunch of niggers between me and the Comanches—"

"Quiet!" a voice roared from inside. "I said you're dismissed, Captain."

The captain turned to leave, but stopped when he saw Ethan.

"Captain Ethan Miller," he said, "as I live and breathe."

"You only get to live and breathe, Colonel Windham," Ethan said, "because I didn't get a chance to put a bullet in your head before the war ended."

"Not a colonel anymore," Windham said. "Not

since Robert E. Lee turned coward on us. Just a lowly captain now, like you were."

"Foley!" a voice called from the office. "Send Captain Akers and Mr. Miller in."

"Yessir!" Foley snapped back. "You can go in, sirs."

"Thank you, Foley," Akers said. "Captain Miller?"

"Still callin' yourself captain are you, Miller?" Windham asked.

Ignoring the comment, Ethan entered the office, followed by Akers, who closed the door firmly behind them.

"Captain Akers," the gray-haired man behind the desk said, "report!"

Ethan listened while Akers reported to Lieutenant Colonel Merritt. This man was about the same age as Windham, but his hair was closer to white than gray.

"And this is Captain Miller, sir," Akers finished. "Captain Miller, this is Lieutenant Colonel Merritt."

"Colonel," Ethan said, "it's just Mr. Miller, now."

"Yes, yes," Merritt said, "please, have a seat, Mr. Miller. Akers, you're dismissed."

"Uh, sir, I thought I'd—"

"Dismissed, Captain!" Merritt snapped.

"Yes, sir."

As Akers left, Merritt seated himself behind his desk. Ethan sat across from the man.

"Colonel, your horses are here and I'd like to be paid."

"Of course," Merritt said, "the herd will just need to be examined and counted, first—"

"And then I get paid?"

"I think, Mr. Miller," Merritt said, donning a pair of wire-framed glasses and picking up a sheet of paper from his desk, "you need to be made aware of some fine print in your contract."

# CHAPTER TWENTY-THREE

"WHAT FINE PRINT?" Ethan asked. "What the hell are you talkin' about? My man Bennett told me you were an honorable man, Colonel."

"I hope he was right, sir," Merritt said. "I wasn't about to let you and your men be chewed to pieces by the Comanches just to save the army money, that's true. But this is right here in black-and-white."

"What is?"

"Are these horses broken and ready to be ridden?" Merritt asked.

"Not at the moment, no," Ethan said. "They're wild horses. Your man Brodie knew that when he came to see them."

"Well, I'm afraid Lieutenant Brodie hadn't read the fine print, either."

"What the hell fine print are you talkin' about, Colonel?" Ethan demanded.

"Right here, it says that you are to deliver two hundred head of horses that are 'suitable for cavalry mounts.'" Merritt took off his glasses and looked at Ethan. "Are they suitable as mounts for my men?"

"Of course they are."

"So that means any one of my men could put a saddle on any one of those horses and ride it?"

"No," Ethan said. "They need to be broke."

"I'm afraid that was your job, Mr. Miller," Merritt said, "not ours."

"Wait a minute," Ethan said, "is this gonna be your way of sayin' I didn't meet the deadline?"

"No, no," Merritt said, "don't misunderstand me. You got the horses here in forty-five days." He folded his hands and set them down on his desk. "I just can't pay you until they're suitable to be ridden."

"So you want me to break all two hundred of them?" Ethan said. "Do you know how long that would take?"

"Well," Merritt said, "your men could be working on that while you're gone. And by the time you get back, it'll be done, and I'll pay you."

"Now what are you blatherin' on about?" Ethan asked. "Where am I goin'?"

"A moment," Merritt said. He walked to the door and opened it. "Foley, where's Sergeant Jackson?"

"He's outside, sir."

"Send him in."

"Yes, sir."

Moments later a large Black man in blue came storming in, hat in hand.

"Colonel, I don't care what you say," he started. "Me and my men ain't about to follow Captain Windham—"

"Sergeant Jackson," Merritt said, loudly, "I want you to meet former Captain Ethan Miller."

Jackson looked at Miller and fell silent for a moment.

"Captain Miller," he said, then. "I heard about you durin' the war, sir."

"I wish I could say the same thing about you, Sergeant," Ethan said. He looked at the colonel. "Merritt, what's goin' on?"

"What's going on, *Mister* Miller," Colonel Merritt said, "is you're about to become Captain Miller, again."

"What?"

"When you mustered out there was a clause that said you could be called back to active duty at a moment's notice."

"Now just a—"

"Sergeant," Merritt said, cutting Ethan off, "if you and your men won't follow Captain Windham, would you follow Captain Miller?"

Jackson fell silent for another moment, then said, "Well, yes, sir. If Captain Miller agreed to lead us, we'd follow."

"Then that's all," Merritt said. "You're dismissed."

"But Colonel—"

"I'll let you know what happens," Merritt said. "You're dismissed."

"Yes, sir."

Jackson looked at Ethan, then put his hat on and left.

"You think I'm gonna put on the uniform again and lead your Buffalo Soldiers on some sort of mission?" Ethan demanded.

"Ah. You know about the Buffalo Soldiers," Merritt said. "Then you should know that even soldiers who fought to free the slaves aren't happy with them being here, in uniform."

"If you order those soldiers to ride with them, they will," Ethan said.

"I can order men to ride together," Merritt said. "That doesn't mean they'll be watching each other's backs."

"You're afraid some of your white soldiers might let some of your Black soldiers get killed?"

Merritt waved his hands.

"We're getting off the subject here, Miller," Merritt said. Ethan noticed he didn't rate a "Captain" or a "Mr." anymore.

"My weapons are out there somewhere," Merritt said. "Weapons and ammunition, and your horses are useless to me without them."

"So send your soldiers out to find them."

"I did," Merritt said. "I've sent two patrols out to find those weapons."

"And?"

"And they haven't come back."

"Comanches?"

"More than likely," Merritt said. "Our blue uniforms can be seen and recognized from far off."

"So send your men out in trail clothes," Ethan said, "not in uniform."

"And that's what you would do?"

"Yes."

Merritt leaned forward, as if wanting to give his words more weight.

"Take it a step further."

The two men stared at each other.

"I get it," Ethan said, finally. "You wanna send out your Buffalo Soldiers in trail clothes. You think the Comanches might leave them alone because they're Black, not white."

"It's possible," Merritt said, "but I need to send an officer with them."

"Like Captain Windham."

"Ah," Merritt said, sitting back in his chair, "but very unlike Captain Windham." He pointed. "That's where you come in."

"I don't wanna come in at all, Colonel," Ethan said.

"Please, Captain, hear me out."

"It's Mister, not Captain," Ethan said. "You have plenty of other officers to send out with your Buffalo Soldiers. Captain Akers seems very competent."

"He is," Merritt said. "All my officers are competent, to one extent or the other."

"Then what's the problem?"

"The problem is, the Black soldiers won't follow them."

"Once again," Ethan said, "if you order them to follow, they will."

"Not with any degree of confidence," Merritt said, "and when push comes to shove out there, it could end up being a disaster."

"So you wanna hold my herd ransom to make me do this," Ethan said.

"Not at all," Merritt said. "The fact of the matter is, the horses need to be broke, and it'll take time. I assume you don't personally break horses at your, uh, age."

Ethan scowled.

"So you'd be sitting around here doing nothing while your men see to the horses," Merritt said. "Why not put yourself to good use?"

"Or get myself killed," Ethan added.

"It's my understanding that these Buffalo Soldiers are good men," Merritt said. "All they need is a good man to follow."

"What makes you think they'll follow me?" Ethan asked.

"You saw Sergeant Jackson's reaction when he realized who you were," Merritt said. "When he tells his men who you are, they'll follow."

Ethan continued to scowl.

"Captain—Mr. Miller," Merritt said, "if we don't get those weapons, we won't be able to hold this fort, or the surrounding area, against the Comanches, the Kiowa, or any tribes."

"What about the other forts?"

"They're in the same situation," Merritt said. "The weapons supply that's coming is for all of us."

"You've got . . . what? Six forts? Why not close one down and distribute their weapons cache among the others?"

"That's a good idea," Merritt admitted, "but not a decision that I can make. It would take a while to get the word from Washington to do that—if they agreed."

"If I was commanding this fort, I wouldn't wait," Ethan said.

"I'm sure you wouldn't," Merritt said, "but then you'd have to convince all the other commanding officers to act without orders."

"You know," Ethan said, "one of the reasons I didn't re-up was because this man's army has no regard for free will."

"Of course it doesn't," Merritt said. "It's the military. It's all about following orders."

"No matter what."

"I'm afraid so," Merritt said. "There are not many officers like you, Captain, who are willing to follow their own gut. But that's just the kind of officer I need right now."

"You're not gonna get me to do this by panderin' to my ego," Ethan warned.

"I believe the only way I can get you to do this," Merritt said, "is to convince you of the importance of the mission."

"And if I don't agree?"

"Then you'll have to spend days, maybe weeks, here while your men break those horses."

Ethan had maybe three men with him who were bronc riders. It would take forever to break two hundred head.

"Can I think about it?" Ethan asked.

"I have to send out a patrol tomorrow to find those weapons," Merritt said. "You can tell me in the morning if they're going out with, or without you. If you decide to accompany them, I'll have your uniform ready for you."

"If I'm goin'," Ethan said, "I won't need a uniform. If the Buffalo Soldiers are going out in trail clothes, that's how I'll go."

"As you wish," Merritt said.


E THAN WENT OUT the rear gate of the fort, which led to the town proper. The first saloon he came to was called Texas Jack's, so he went inside. Sure enough, most of his men were in there, quenching their forty-five days' thirst.

He saw Taggart and Granger sitting at a table together, got a beer from the bar, and walked over to join them.

"There's the moneyman," Granger said, happily. "We're almost ready for you to buy the next round."

"You might hafta wait awhile," Ethan said.

"What d'ya mean, boss?" Taggart asked.

"You didn't get paid?" Granger asked.

"That's what I mean," Ethan said, sipping his beer.

"What's goin' on, Ethan?" Granger asked.

He explained the situation to them.

# CHAPTER TWENTY-FOUR

"I KNEW THEY'D TRY somethin'," Granger spat when Ethan finished.

"Now, hang on," Taggart said. "Does it say that in the contract, or doesn't it?"

"I assume it does," Ethan said.

"Where's your copy, boss?" Taggart asked.

"In my saddlebags."

"Well, why don't you take a look at it tonight," Taggart said, "and then go from there."

Ethan looked around at his hands, who were drinking and laughing.

"We better tell them to save their money," Ethan said, "plus we'll be campin' outside the gates, and not stayin' in a hotel."

"There are no stores in the chuck wagon to feed the men," Granger said.

"Akers said they'd replenish us," Ethan said. "Let's you and me find him."

"That leaves me to give the men the good news," Taggart said. "Thanks."

Granger grinned at him.

"You're the foreman."


E THAN AND GRANGER found Captain Akers inside the fort, in the officer's quarters.

"If I had known the CO was going to pull that, I would've warned you," Akers said.

"I appreciate that," Ethan said, "but right now we just need to feed our men tonight."

"Bring your chuck wagon right around to the front gate and I'll have it loaded. I know your men will be camping out tonight, but we can make room for you in here, Captain."

Ethan looked around at the interior of the officers' barracks. There were half a dozen beds, some tables and chairs, and a potbellied stove.

"Captain Windham'll be in here tonight, won't he?" Ethan asked.

"I'm afraid so," Akers said.

"Then I'll stay outside with my men," Ethan said. "But thanks for the offer."

"I'll get right on those supplies," Akers said. He and Ethan left the barracks together.

Granger was waiting outside.

"Captain Akers is gonna see to the supplies," Ethan told him. "We need to get the chuck wagon around to the gate."

"I'll go find Moze and Abraham," Granger said.

"They won't be in a saloon," Ethan said. "Try the Buffalo Soldier's barracks."

"Good idea."

"I'm goin' back to that saloon for a whiskey, but I'm gonna get my saddlebags first."

"Meet ya there," Granger said, and they split up.

* * *

B ACK AT TEXAS JACK'S, Ethan ordered a shot of whiskey
and a beer, then took them—and his saddlebags—to
a table. His men were still drinking, but rather morosely
rather than happily, so he assumed they had gotten the
news.

He took out the contract he had signed and began
reading. By the time Granger and Taggart joined him,
he had read the section twice.

"So?" Granger asked. "What's it say?"

"Just what the colonel said," Ethan replied.

"So, if they wanna get particular—" Taggart said.

"Which apparently they do," Granger inserted.

"—they can hold you to it," Taggart ended.

"Damn it!" Ethan said.

"I'll get the next round," Granger said. "Beers all
around?"

Ethan and Taggart nodded.

"You gonna do it, boss?" Taggart asked, after Granger
went to the bar.

"I don't know," Ethan said. "Colonel Merritt sounded
pretty desperate. And he did send his men out to get us."

"He sent them to get the herd," Taggart pointed out.

"He could've waited till mornin', like Windham
suggested," Ethan said. "He didn't."

"So you're gonna risk your life for him?" Taggart
asked.

"It wouldn't be for him," Ethan said. "If he tried to
send those Buffalo Soldiers out there with Windham
as their CO, they'll all get killed. And if he doesn't get
those weapons to distribute to this and the other forts,
they're gonna fall to the Comanches. Then the settlers
will be next."

"Sounds like you're talkin' yourself into it," Taggart
said.

"I may need to talk to one more person before I decide," Ethan said.

"Who?"

"His name's Jackson."


E THAN FOUND THE barracks that had been assigned to the Buffalo Soldiers. It was little more than a shack, with twenty men stuffed into it.

"What you want?" a huge Black man asked him at the door.

"I'm Ethan Miller. I'd like to see Sergeant Jackson."

"You Cap'n Miller?" the man asked.

"That's right."

"Wait here."

The big Black man went inside, closing the door behind him. When the door opened again, Ezekial Jackson stood there.

"Captain Miller," he said, "what can I do for you?"

"We need to talk," Ethan said.

Jackson stepped out, closed the door behind him. Not as big as the Black man who had answered the door, he still towered over Ethan.

"Let's walk," Jackson said.

Together, they started away from the building.

"You deserve better quarters than that," Ethan said.

"Yeah, we do," Jackson said. "But we're gonna have to earn it."

"Is that why you're goin' out after those weapons?" Ethan asked.

"Partly," Jackson said.

"What's the other part?"

"Orders," Jackson said. "We're in the army, and we gotta follow orders."

"Do all your men feel that way?"

"Yessir."

"What about following Captain Windham?" Ethan asked. "If you were ordered to follow him, would you all do it?"

"We'd do it," Jackson said. "We wouldn't be happy about it, but we'd do it. But once we got out there, I don't know what would happen. I don't think we could blindly follow his orders."

"So whose orders *would* you blindly follow?" Ethan asked.

"Somebody we trusted, and believed in," Jackson said.

Ethan didn't really want to hear the next word, but it came.

"You!" Jackson said. "We would follow you, Captain."

"Why me?" Ethan asked.

"Most of us heard about you during the war," Jackson said. "I don't think when you look at us you'll see a bunch of niggers in blue uniforms. I think you'll see soldiers."

"Even if we ain't in uniforms?"

Jackson grinned.

"Even if we ain't in uniforms."

Ethan looked up, saw that they were standing in front of the officers' barracks.

"How about this?" Ethan asked. "How about I make it a condition that when we get back, you and your men get a larger barracks. Maybe even this one."

Jackson smiled, showing slightly yellowed teeth.

"And that we get back alive," he said.

"Yes," Ethan said. "That, too."

E THAN WALKED JACKSON back to the cramped barracks.

"My men are good men, Captain," Jackson said. "They'll follow you, and obey orders."

"Who was that big one who answered the door?"
Ethan asked.

"That's my cousin Gabriel."

"Have any of your men fought Indians before?"
Ethan asked.

"No, sir," Jackson said. "We haven't fought the red
man, only the white man."

"Well," Ethan said, "then that gives you something
in common with the Comanches."

"Have you fought Indians, Captain?" Jackson asked.
"Since the war?"

"Once or twice, Sergeant," Ethan said. "Once or
twice. But I have a man who has more experience than
I do."

"Will he come, too?" Jackson asked.

"I'm gonna ask 'im," Ethan said, "as soon as I've
made up my mind, for sure."

"Seems to me you already have, Captain," Jackson
said, "but we'll wait to hear in the morning."

Jackson threw Ethan a salute, and went into the
barracks.

Ethan turned and headed for the front gate. His
men were camped just outside. Fires were going; Moze
and Abraham were cooking.

As he approached the camp Granger walked to
meet him.

"Captain Akers kept his word," he told Ethan.
"Abraham has a stew goin'."

"Good."

"And we've got plenty of water."

They walked into camp together.

"Are all the men here?" Ethan asked.

"Yeah," Granger said, "we all left the saloon when
we ran out of money."

"That's gonna have to be another condition," Ethan
said.

"What's that?"

"If I decide to go, I'll need each man to be given a stipend," Ethan said. "They're gonna hafta be able to live while we're gone."

"Hey, wait . . . we?" Granger asked. "While *we're* gone?"

"We need to talk, Grange."

GRANGER LISTENED TO Ethan's pitch without saying a word. When Ethan finished talking, his friend stared at him for a few moments.

"Why me?" he finally asked.

"You know the answer to that," Ethan said. "I need somebody I can trust. And you have experience with Indians."

"Years ago, Ethan," Granger said. "Before the war."

"Still," Ethan said, "more than I have. You've been invaluable this trip when it came to dealin' with the Apaches, and the Comanches."

"So you, me, and twenty Buffalo Soldiers?"

"That's right."

"Do I have to wear a uniform?"

"No," Ethan said, "none of us will be wearin' uniforms."

"And you're gonna be reinstated?" Granger said. "Do I hafta be?"

"Neither of us," Ethan said. "That'll be another condition. We'll be civilian hires."

# CHAPTER TWENTY-FIVE

"YOU WHAT?" TAGGART asked at breakfast the next morning.

"I'm takin' Grange with me," Ethan said.

Taggart looked at Granger.

"You agreed to this?"

"I can't let him go and get killed," Granger said.

Taggart looked at Ethan.

"Then why not take more of us?"

"No," Ethan said, "I don't want to risk anyone else's life. Besides, you're gonna have work to do, here."

"Breakin' the horses," Taggart said.

"Right. I want them all broke by the time we come back, so we can get paid and out of here."

"You're sure you'll be comin' back?" Taggart asked.

"George," Ethan said, "we made it through the war, we'll make it through this."

"I just hope you're right," Taggart said.

"But just in case," Ethan said, "if we don't come back, Paradise is yours."

"What?"

"That is," Ethan added, "if you want it."

"You're talkin' crazy," Taggart said. "That ranch is somethin' you talked about all durin' the war."

"That's why if anythin' happens to me, I want you and the men to have it."

"And what if you get killed, but Grange comes back?" Taggart asked.

"That ain't gonna matter," Granger said. "I don't want the ranch. I'll just stay on and work for you."

"This whole thing is crazy," Taggart said. "You do what you gotta do, Ethan. I'll get the men busy breaking broncs."

"I've gotta go and see the colonel," Ethan said.

"I'm gonna sit right here and drink coffee," Granger said. "You just tell me when we're leavin'."

"That's gonna depend on how Colonel Merritt reacts to my conditions."

As Ethan walked away Taggart looked at Granger.

"Why's he doin' this?"

"Maybe," Granger said, "he'd rather have somethin' to do than sit around and think about how some fine print got the better of 'im."

"If we hadn't come so far, and gone through so much," Taggart said, "I'd tell the army what to do with their fine print."

Granger just nodded and drank his coffee.

L IEUTENANT FOLEY BROUGHT Ethan into Colonel Merritt's office.

"Coffee?" Merritt asked.

"Sure."

"Lieutenant," Merritt said, "bring coffee."

"Yes, sir."

As Foley left Merritt said, "Have a seat."

Ethan sat across from the man, who settled down behind his desk.

"Have you made up your mind?" he asked.

"Pretty much."

"Good."

"There are just some conditions I'll need met."

"And what would those be?"

Ethan told the colonel about the stipend he wanted for his men, and the new barracks for the Buffalo Soldiers. While he was talking Foley came in with a tray and set it down on the colonel's desk. Merritt and Ethan each got their own coffee.

"Is that it?" Merritt asked.

"Not quite," Ethan said. "I'll be takin' one of my men with us."

"Who would that be?"

"Granger."

"Sergeant Granger, if I remember correctly."

"He was a sergeant, yes," Ethan said.

"I can arrange for him to be re—"

"No," Ethan said, "neither one of us wants to be reinstated."

"You're going to be in command of an army troop," Merritt said.

"Put Sergeant Jackson in command," Ethan said. "Granger and I will be civilian hires."

"You mean, like scouts?"

"Sure," Ethan said, "if you have to call us somethin', call us civilian scouts."

"Are you going to want to meet with your men?" Merritt asked.

"I talked with Jackson last night," Ethan said. "I'll get to know the rest of the men on the way."

"All right," Merritt said, "I'll have horses saddled for you—"

"Granger and me, we'll use our own horses," Ethan

said, standing up. "Have the Ninth saddled and ready out front in an hour."

"They'll be there," Merritt said. "These conditions of yours, do you want them in writing?"

"Unlike the army," Ethan said, "I'm gonna take you at your word, Colonel."

ETHAN AND GRANGER saddled their horses and checked their weapons. Not wanting any pack animals slowing them down, Ethan had Abraham fill two gunnysacks with provisions. One was hanging from each of their saddles.

Confident he was leaving the bronc-busting job in good hands with Taggart, Ethan was sure the man would get the job done.

The men wished them luck as they rode out of camp, with Taggart shaking hands with each of them.

When they reached the colonel's office, the Buffalo Soldiers were gathered in front, some mounted, others standing. The adjutant, Foley, was standing among them, and when he saw Ethan and Granger he stepped inside. Moments later, Colonel Merritt came out.

The two men dismounted and walked over to him. Sergeant Jackson joined them.

"Do we all understand the situation?" Merritt said.

"Yessir," Jackson said. "I'm in charge of my men, but we're following the captain and his man."

"Not Captain, Jackson," Ethan said. "Me and Granger are civilians."

Jackson looked at his men, and then at Ethan.

"You're gonna be Captain to us, sir," he said.

"Fine," Ethan said, then turned to Merritt. "You've got to have some idea where these weapons are, Colonel. We can't go out there and just wander around."

"They were taken off a train in Houston and loaded onto wagons. They've got to be someplace between here and there."

"So we're talkin' . . . " Ethan said, and looked at Granger.

"About six hundred miles," he said. "Some folks call it the Sagebrush Trail."

"We got word that they made it to San Antonio," Merritt said.

"So now we're down to four hundred miles," Granger said.

"What kind of an escort did they have?"

"One full troop," Merritt said.

"Jesus, that's thirty, forty men. So you're figurin' Comanches, or Kiowa, or some other tribe intercepted the weapons," Ethan said to Merritt, "and took them away from forty armed soldiers?"

"That's one possibility."

"What's the other one?" Ethan asked. "The one you've kept from me, until now."

"Well, as you know, there are many Confederate veterans who won't accept that the South lost the war. Some of them are riding in bands, trying to wreak havoc on what they still consider to be the Union. There is one such band roaming South Texas."

"So you think some ex-Confederate soldiers might have the weapons."

"It's possible."

"Do we have any idea who's leadin' this band of would-be Quantrill's Raiders?"

"That's the odd part," Merritt said. "Their leader wasn't a grayback, he was a blue belly. His name's Ashforth. Calls himself Colonel Ashforth."

"Ashforth!" Granger spat. "That sonofabitch?"

"You know him?" Merritt asked.

"Colonel, you're gonna tell me, when you offered me this assignment, you didn't know that *Lieutenant* Ashforth was my second durin' the war?"

"I had no idea," Merritt said. "Does this change things?"

"It does for me," Granger said. "I'm gonna find that son of a bitch and put a bullet in his gut."

Ethan turned to Jackson.

"Are your men outfitted like we talked about last night, Sergeant?"

"Yes, sir," Jackson said. "We won't be needing any pack animals."

"That's good," Ethan said. "Let's mount up."

"Yes, sir."

Jackson turned to face his men and shouted, "Mount up!"

But before they could leave, an irate-looking officer came storming over to where they were standing.

"Talk about graybacks," Jackson muttered.

Captain Franklin Windham looked like he was breathing fire, and Ethan wondered if the man had spent the morning drinking. His uniform was soiled, his shirt hung outside his trousers.

"You won't get away with this, *Colonel* Merritt!" he shouted.

"Stand down, Captain!" Merritt snapped. "You're bucking for a stay in the stockade."

"This is my troop," Windham went on. "These niggers report to me! I should be leading them."

"Be my guest," Ethan said. "I'll gladly step down—"

"You'll do no such thing!" Merritt shouted. "Captain, get yourself together."

"If I was in command of this fort—"

"But you're not," Merritt interrupted, "and thank God for that." Merritt turned to his adjutant. "Lieutenant Foley, have Captain Windham escorted back to his barracks. If he resists, then take him to the stockade."

"Yes, sir!"

Foley gave the order and several men snapped to and marched the captain away while he was still belly-aching.

"Ready to go?" Merritt asked.

"No," Ethan said.

"What now?" Merritt asked. "Another condition?"

"No," Ethan said, "I wanna talk to Windham."

"About what?" Merritt asked.

"If it was Ashforth and his band who took the weapons," Ethan said, "how did they know about them? They needed some inside information. Where they came from, where they were goin', and how many men were escortin' them."

"And you think Windham told them?" Merritt asked.

"We're talkin' about disgruntled soldiers who ain't happy with the way the war went," Ethan said. "That includes Ashforth and Windham."

Merritt rubbed his jaw.

"You have a point," he said.

"So let me talk to him before we leave," Ethan said. "It would help if we knew who we were after."

Merritt turned to Foley.

"Take Captain Miller to the officers' barracks. See that he's not disturbed while talking with Captain Windham."

"You want me to come with you?" Granger asked.

"No," Ethan said, pointing at Sergeant Jackson, "I want him."

# CHAPTER TWENTY-SIX

Ethan not only took Jackson with him, but the sergeant's cousin Gabriel. When they entered the barracks he had a huge Black man on either side of him.

"What's this?" Windham said, standing up.

"I've got some questions for you, Captain," Ethan said. "If I don't like the answers, my friends here have permission to loosen your tongue."

"You wouldn't dare," Windham said. "I'm an officer."

"I can have you busted to private in a minute," Ethan said. "Then these two men would outrank you."

Ezekial and Gabriel took one step toward Windham, who appeared frail by comparison.

"What do you want to know?" the man asked.

"Did you pass on the information about the weapons to *Colonel* Ashforth and his band?"

"Who?"

"Come on," Ethan said. "Colonel Anthony Ashforth, formerly known as Lieutenant Ashforth of the Union Army."

"The man who's leading a band of Confederate expatriates?" Windham asked. "How would I know him?"

"Come on, Windham," Ethan said, "if anyone hates what Robert E. Lee did at Appomattox, it's you."

"You're right," Windham said. "I think it was a cowardly act. What's that got to do with me helping someone steal a cache of weapons?"

"Because Ashforth would be fixin' to use those weapons to rearm the Confederacy. It's my guess you'd be right there with that idea."

"Well, if you think that, you might as well let these two big bull niggers kill me right now. Go ahead. Because I'm tellin' you I don't know the man, and I don't know anything about those weapons being stolen. I may hate bein' a captain in this army, but it's all I've got now, Miller." Windham sat heavily on his bed, his suspenders falling to either side. "All I've got."

"Sir?" Jackson said to Ethan.

"Yes, Sergeant?"

"I know you didn't ask me, sir," Jackson said, "but I believe 'im."

Ethan looked at the two Black men, and then back at the remnants of what was, at one time, a proud Confederate officer.

"That's the problem, Sergeant," he said. "I believe him, too."

E THAN WALKED BACK with Ezekial and Gabriel Jackson to where the Buffalo Soldiers were waiting, in front of the CO's office. Colonel Merritt was still standing just outside the front door.

"Well?"

"He's a broken man, Colonel," Ethan said, "but I

doubt he has anythin' to do with the weapons missin', or with Ashforth's raiders."

"Well," Merritt said, "nevertheless, I'll keep an eye on him while you're gone."

Ethan walked over to Granger.

"No luck?" his friend asked.

"No," Ethan said. "That's just a sad, sad man, holdin' on to what he has left."

"Which ain't much, I'd guess," Granger said.

"Are you ready to roll out, Captain?" Merritt asked Ethan.

"We're ready, sir," Ethan said.

He turned and saw that Jackson already had the men mounted up. He and Granger did the same.

"We're gonna need somebody to scout on head of us, Sergeant," he said.

"Yes, sir," Jackson said. "That would be Noah—uh, I mean, Private Jackson."

"Another cousin, Sergeant?"

Sergeant Jackson smiled broadly.

"Oh, yes sir."

"Well, get 'im out there ahead of us, then."

"Yes, sir."

Private Noah Jackson led the way out the front gate, with Ethan, Granger, and the Buffalo Soldiers following. They rode past the Paradise crew's camp. Taggart and the men saluted.


AFTER THEY HAD ridden a few miles Granger reached out a hand to Ethan for him to stop.

"Keep goin'," Ethan told Sergeant Jackson. "We'll catch up."

"Yes, sir."

As the Buffalo Soldiers continued on, Ethan turned to Granger.

"What's on your mind?" he asked.

"Where the hell are we goin'?" Granger asked. "I mean, I know what we're supposed to be doin', but . . . we've got four hundred miles to cover. How do we do that?"

"Well," Ethan said "we could go directly to Houston, and then work our way back."

"That'd take a week, maybe more," Granger said.

"How long is it gonna take our boys to break two hundred head?" Ethan asked. "We've got time to kill."

"Is that all we're doin'?" Granger asked. "Killin' time?"

"Do you think we have a chance in hell of findin' those weapons?" Ethan asked.

Granger looked shocked.

"You mean you took this assignment knowin' we weren't ever gonna succeed?"

"Whether we succeed or not," Ethan said, "these soldiers are gonna get better treatment when they return. And our boys are bein' taken care of while they break those horses."

"So what do we do while we're out here?"

"Go through the motions," Ethan said. "Those weapons could be anywhere within four hundred miles. But what if we go lookin' for Ashforth?"

"And his raiders?"

"Why not?"

"Okay, how do we start?"

"What's the biggest town to the east?" Ethan asked.

"That'd be . . . Sheffield," Granger said.

"How far?"

"About a hundred and eighty miles," Granger said, "but we'll have to pass Fort Stockton, first."

"How far's that?"

"About halfway."

"Good," Ethan said. "We'll ride for a while today

and stop at Fort Stockton. Maybe they'll have some information about where Ashforth and his men were seen last."

"We won't make it today," Granger said, "but we can camp, and get there tomorrow afternoon."

"Sounds good."

"And what do we tell these fellers?" Granger asked, indicating the Buffalo Soldiers ahead of them. "Do we tell 'em this is all for show?"

"No," Ethan said, "we just tell 'em what we need to, day by day."

"Do you think the colonel really thinks we can find those weapons?"

"I think Colonel Merritt just keeps playin' the cards he's dealt," Ethan said.

"He don't know he got dealt two jokers this time, does he?" Granger asked.

"Hell, no, he don't," Ethan said.


THEY CAMPED FOR the night, built two fires. Noah Jackson cooked over one of the fires, and everybody got some beans and coffee.

Sergeant Jackson came over with his plate and cup then sat with Ethan and Granger.

"If you don't mind, sirs," he said, just before his butt hit the ground.

"Not at all, Sergeant," Ethan said.

"What's our count, Sergeant?" Ethan asked Jackson.

"There's twenty of us, Captain," Jackson said. "Plus you and you, Sergeant, we got twenty-two."

"And how many cousins?" Ethan asked.

Jackson grinned.

"Just the two, sir, Gabriel and Noah."

"The count might be enough to discourage any Comanche huntin' parties, sir," Granger said.

"That's good," Ethan said.

"If you don't mind me asking, sir," Jackson said.

"Go ahead."

"Where are we heading?"

"East, Sergeant," Ethan said.

"I know that much, sir," Jackson said, "but where are we going to look for those weapons?"

"We'll be comin' to Fort Stockton tomorrow," Ethan said. "We'll ask some questions there, and then continue on to Sheffield. Same thing there. Questions, and then we press on."

"And we keep on going that way until . . . what?"

"Until we find the weapons, or we get to Houston," Ethan said. "Personally, I'm hoping we don't get all the way to Houston."

Jackson fell silent.

"Is that gonna satisfy your men when you tell 'em, Sergeant?" Ethan asked.

"I suppose it'll have to, sir, won't it?"

"If we encounter that self-appointed Colonel Ashforth along the way," Granger said "there'll be some fightin'."

"You fellas knew him during the war?"

"Oh, we knew 'im," Granger said. "And even then I woulda been chuckwagon glad to put a bullet in 'im."

"He wasn't a good soldier?" Jackson asked.

"He was a terrible soldier," Granger said.

"Then why does he want to continue the war?" Jackson asked.

"Remember what Windham said, back in Fort Davis?" Ethan asked.

"That the army was all he had?" Jackson asked.

"I'm, thinkin' that pretty much sums up what Ashforth feels, too," Ethan said. "That he hasn't got anythin' else."

"I guess we can understand that," Jackson said.

"You and your cousins, you mean?" Ethan asked.

"All my men," Jackson said. "Ain't too many of us got anything else."

"That's a shame."

"You feel that way, sir?"

"Not at all," Ethan said. "That's why I started Paradise, my ranch, up in Montana Territory. That's why I drove my herd here, hoping to get paid. Once I get paid, I'll have somethin' to go back to."

"I envy you, sir." Jackson took his plate and cup, stood and walked back to his men.

Granger dropped his fork in his plate and said, "I miss our chuck wagon."

THE NEXT AFTERNOON they arrived at the gates of Fort Stockton, which weren't immediately opened to them. Ethan was admitted, and once he showed his orders to General Edward Hatch, the gates were open. Ethan's men were allowed to water their horses and refill their own canteens.

Ethan accompanied General Hatch to his office. The General was obviously an experienced soldier, and while he had a healthy white mustache, the hair on his head had been left behind on many battlefields, until he had nothing but a pink scalp.

"Have a seat, Captain Miller," Hatch said. "I didn't mean to doubt you. In fact, we have a troop of our own Buffalo Soldiers here. I just never saw so many of them out of uniform. Is there a reason for that?"

"Yes, sir," Ethan said. "We felt the Comanches might not have any reason to attack a group of Black men—that is, as long as they're not wearing blue uniforms."

"I suppose that's a good point," Hatch said. "Now, what can I do for you?"

"You can fill me in on the Comanche activity in this

area, and also let me know if you've heard anything about Colonel Ashforth and his men."

"Is Merritt thinkin' those weapons were stolen by a bunch of disgruntled ex-Confederates?"

"A frustrated officer like Ashforth might think he could restart a war with those weapons," Ethan observed.

"I thought they were just a ragtag group of ex-soldiers," Hatch said.

"I'm gonna try and find out if that's true, sir," Ethan said.

"Well," Hatch said, "we haven't heard anythin' about him bein' in the area, but I can certainly tell you about the Comanches."

Hatch stood up and pointed to the map on the wall behind his desk . . .

# CHAPTER TWENTY-SEVEN

GENERAL HATCH OFFERED to put them all up for the night in the fort, but Ethan turned him down.

"I think we'd like to keep goin'," he said. "There's no point in gettin' too comfortable. Thank you for the information."

"Of course."

Hatch walked Ethan out to where the Buffalo Soldiers were mounted once again.

"Do you need any supplies?" Hatch asked.

Ethan mounted up.

"We only left Fort Davis yesterday, General," he said. "We should be fine."

"Well then, I wish you luck."

Ethan took the lead and led the men through the front gate, which closed behind them.

"Captain, do you want me to send Noah up ahead of us, again?" Sergeant Jackson asked.

"I don't think so, Sergeant," Ethan said. "I think he

might be more valuable as a cook. Let's keep together today."

"Yes, sir."

Ethan didn't want to send one or even two men ahead of the rest, recalling what had happened to his man, Treadway. While he didn't imagine the Comanches would attack twenty Black men, he didn't want to take the chance that they would attack two.

"Let's figure there's more safety in numbers," Ethan added.

"Yes, sir."

"But put Noah at the head of the column, anyway," Ethan said. "He can ride with Granger, and you ride with me. The rest can ride in a column of two behind us. And let's keep a sharp eye out for anybody showin' an interest in us."

"Yes, sir."

Jackson rode up and down, whipping the men into a column led by Noah and Granger. Then he came back to ride alongside Ethan.

"What did you find out from the general?" he asked.

"There's been no sign of Ashforth in the area, but the Comanches have been raidin', attacking travelers and settlers, alike."

"And the weapons?"

"Not in the hands of the Comanches," Ethan said. "There's been no report of Indians with rifles."

"So we're back to thinking it was Ashforth who stole them?" Jackson asked.

"Or some third party," Ethan said. "Maybe Comancheros."

"I ain't heard anything about Comancheros in the area," Jackson said.

"Maybe Mexican bandits, then, comin' across the border," Ethan offered.

"Then why wouldn't they be taking the weapons back to Mexico with them, for their own war?"

"We're not worried about them usin' the weapons against us," Ethan said. "Merritt says all the forts need those weapons to combat the Indians."

"Why don't the colonel just contact Washington and ask for more weapons?"

"He hasn't said so," Ethan said, "but I doubt he wants Washington to know the weapons have gone missin'."

"Then he ain't going to want to know that it was us who got them back," Jackson said.

"That may not be true," Ethan said. "After all, you're all soldiers."

Both men looked over when Granger came riding back to them.

"What is it?" Ethan asked.

"Comanches," Granger said. "They're watchin' us."

"How many?" Ethan asked.

"We only saw two," Granger said.

"How were they armed?" Ethan asked.

"Bow and arrow," Granger said. "We didn't see any rifles."

"Well," Ethan said, "if they wanna watch us, let 'em watch. Like we figured, there may be too many of us for them to attack."

"Unless they get some help," Granger said.

"We'll hafta wait and see," Ethan said. "For now we'll just keep headin' for Sheffield."

"We can make it by tomorrow afternoon," Granger said.

"Maybe the law there will know somethin'."

Granger nodded, rode back ahead to ride alongside Noah.

"You haven't fought Indians before?" Ethan asked Jackson.

"I came right here from Philadelphia, where I lived after the war," Jackson said. "I've never even seen an Indian up close."

"What were you doin' in Philadelphia?" Ethan asked.

"I was thinking about becoming a lawyer," Jackson said.

"What changed your mind?"

"Money," Jackson said. "I didn't have any. So I signed up with the army again, and they sent me out here."

"You savin' your money to go to law school?" Ethan asked.

"That's the idea."

"What about your cousins?"

"They didn't have any other family back East, so they signed up with me. We all got sent out here."

"If none of you have fought Indians, why did you send Noah out as a scout?"

"That's what he did in the war," Jackson said. "He was real good at seeing what was going on, without being seen."

"Well," Ethan said, "we've all been seen, now."

Jackson looked around.

"Don't do that," Ethan said.

"I don't see anybody."

"They're out there," Ethan said. "Just don't look like you're worried about it. Noah and Granger will keep their eyes peeled."

"I don't want my first contact with a Comanche to be at the point of an arrow," Jackson said.

"Can't blame you for that," Ethan said, "but if that was what they wanted to do, they woulda done it by now. No, right now they're just watchin'."

"For what?" Jackson asked.

"We'll find out," Ethan said, "sooner or later."

* * *

THEY CAMPED AGAIN that night, built two fires again. Noah cooked while Ethan set two-man watches. After they had all eaten their beans, he had the first two men relieved so they could eat.

"When we turn in," Granger said, "I'll take a watch with one of the Buffalo Soldiers."

"Take Gabriel," Ezekial Jackson said. "He could learn a lot from you."

"If you say so, Sarge," Granger agreed.

As the Buffalo Soldiers turned in, Ethan noticed the difference between this camp and the camps they made during the trail drive. These men were all quiet, and there didn't seem to be as much camaraderie.

"Ezekial," Ethan said, "did these men all know each other before they came here?"

"No, sir," Jackson said. "Only me and my cousins knew each other. All the others met when we all got here."

"I see."

"But I've known them long enough to know that they're all good men, Captain."

"I'll take your word for that," Ethan said.

"Whether we have to fight white men, or red, they'll follow every one of your orders. Those of them who were slaves know you fought to free them."

"I was just one of many," Ethan said.

"Everyone knew you—"

"Let's not talk about the war, okay, Ezekial? It's in the past."

"Not if this Colonel Ashforth has anything to say about it."

"Good point."

"You never did say how you knew him."

"He was my second-in-command," Ethan explained.

"I thought that was Sergeant Granger."

"Grange would've been, if he had let me promote him, but he never wanted to be an officer. So I was stuck with Ashforth."

"And he wasn't a good officer?"

"He was terrible," Ethan said. "He wasn't fighting to free the slaves, he was fighting just to fight. It doesn't surprise me that he's put on Confederate Gray to continue his own private little war. He's a sick, sick man."

"Well, maybe we can put an end to his war while we're out here."

"That would be a bonus to recoverin' those weapons," Ethan said.

"Would you like more coffee, sir?" Jackson asked. "I'm going to get some."

"Sure, thanks."

The big Black man walked to the coffee pot, poured two cups, and carried them back. Beyond him Ethan could see Granger and Gabriel in conversation. Gabriel towered over the white man.

"Tell me about your cousins," Ethan said, when Jackson returned. "What was Gabriel doin' before the war?"

"Fighting," Ezekial said. "In the ring. He was a bare-knuckle fighter."

"He must've been good."

"Undefeated in eighty-one fights," Ezekial said, proudly.

"Was he a champion?"

Ezekial shook his head.

"Both Joe Coburn and Jimmy Elliott refused to fight him. They were afraid."

"I can't say I blame them," Ethan said. "He's . . . imposing."

"Six-foot-eight," Ezekial said. "I'm six-five, and he makes me feel small."

"You ever fight him?"

"All the time, when we were kids," Ezekial said. "He whipped me every time. As an adult I've been too smart to ever go up against him."

"What about Noah?" Ethan asked. "What's his story?"

"Noah was born a slave," Ezekial said. "It was the war that freed him, and when he came north our family took him in. He worked as a cook, a blacksmith, a carpenter . . . he has a lot of talents."

"Including a scout?"

"When the plantation he lived on was burned out, Noah managed to join the Union Army, while he was still, legally, a slave. He's a smart boy, and learned a lot."

"Then I'm glad to have you and your cousins along," Ethan said.

"I'm only hoping the army will recognize how valuable all these men are," Ezekial Jackson said. "Maybe this assignment will do it. At least it got us away from Captain Windham. He hates Blacks, whether we're slaves or free."

"Sounds like he and Ashforth are the same person," Ethan said. "It still wouldn't surprise me if he was Ashforth's inside man, but I have to say, I believed him when he pleaded his case."

"I did, too," Jackson said.

"We better turn in, Ezekial," Ethan said.

"I told Gabriel to wake me to spell him," Ezekial Jackson said.

"I suppose I should take a watch, as well," Ethan offered.

"No, sir," Ezekial Jackson said. "You're the captain. We need you to be sharp and well rested. You let us take care of the watch."

"Okay, Sergeant," Ethan said. "You've got a deal."

# CHAPTER TWENTY-EIGHT

They made Sheffield the next afternoon. All morning and afternoon they had been watched by the two Comanches. As they rode into town they attracted a lot of attention. The people of Sheffield had obviously never seen twenty Black men riding down their main street.

Ethan had explained to Sergeant Ezekial Jackson that they didn't want any trouble in Sheffield. He simply wanted to talk with the local law and see what he might find out. He considered leaving all the men outside of town and riding in alone, but felt that might show a lack of respect for them. So he just took the lead and the Buffalo Soldiers followed him into town in a column of twos.

He spotted the local sheriff's office as they rode down the main street, reined in his horse in front of it. He looked at Granger and Jackson. "I shouldn't be long."

"I could take the boys over to that saloon across the street for a beer," Granger offered.

Ethan studied the men. They all looked dusty and parched, and could probably use a beer.

"Try to stay out of trouble, Grange," he said to his friend, who understood he meant "Keep everyone out of trouble."

As he dismounted, the door to the office opened and a man wearing a badge stepped out. He looked to be about fifty, wore a gun like he knew how to use it.

"These niggers all belong to you?" he asked Ethan.

"They belong to the United States Army," Ethan said. "They're all soldiers."

"Is that right?" the sheriff asked. "Negro soldiers?"

"That's right."

"And who are you?"

"If we can go into your office," Ethan said, "I'll explain the situation."

The sheriff watched as all the Black men dismounted and followed Granger over to the Palace Saloon, across the street.

"Come on in, then," he said, and opened the door again.

Ethan followed him in and closed the door behind them. The lawman got behind the small wooden desk that was leaning because it had only three legs. Behind him was a gun rack, half filled with rifles and shotguns.

"My name's Ethan Miller," Ethan began.

"Sheriff Ralph Colby," the man said. "What's on your mind Mr. Miller? It's *Mister* Miller? You're not a soldier?"

"I was, at one time," Ethan said. "I've been recruited to lead these Buffalo Soldiers on a mission."

"What kind of mission?"

"A shipment of weapons has gone missin'," Ethan said. "We've been sent out to try and locate them."

"And what do you think happened to these weapons?"

"Could be anythin'," Ethan said. "Comanches, Kiowa, maybe Comancheros."

"Well," the sheriff said, "there's plenty of them redskins in the area."

"And there's another possibility," Ethan said.

"What's that?"

"Do you know a man named Colonel Ashforth?"

"Ashforth's Raiders?" Sheriff Colby said. "Sure, a bunch of graybacks who don't wanna admit the war is over. They been raidin' all over Texas."

"They might figure with a shipment of weapons they can restart the war," Ethan said. "Have you heard of any activity by them in the area?"

"Actually," Colby said, "I have. There's a town south of here called Valverde. It's on what used to be called the Sagebrush Trail. But that kind of disappeared after the Texas Pecos Trail was founded."

"I know Valverde," Ethan said. "Stanley's Brigade fought there during the war, at the Battle of Valverde."

"I heard that Ashforth was seen in that area," Colby said.

"That makes sense," Ethan said. "It's the sight of a rare Confederate victory in Texas."

"That's what I thought."

"You wouldn't happen to have gone down there, would you?" Ethan asked.

"Out of my jurisdiction," Colby said.

"How long ago did you hear this?"

"Oh, a coupla months. I was thinkin' maybe that was where Ashforth was makin' his headquarters."

"That's mighty helpful information, Sheriff," Ethan said.

"Well, I'm all for helpin' the army, Mr. Miller. You mind if I ask what your rank was in the military?"

"Captain," Ethan said, "I was a Captain."

"Well, Captain," Colby said, "while I don't mind

you and your men stoppin' in my town, we've got a mix of Union and Confederate sympathizers here. I'd appreciate it if you could get your men out of here before there's any unpleasantness."

"That's what I'm gonna try to do, Sheriff," Ethan said. "But first I'm gonna join my men across the street for one beer to wash away the trail dust, and then we'll be on our way."

"I'd be much obliged, Captain."

Ethan nodded, touched the brim of his hat, and left the office.

WHEN HE WALKED over to the Palace Saloon he saw Gabriel standing outside with the horses.

"Why ain't you inside havin' a beer, Gabriel?" Ethan asked.

"Cap'n, I don't drink," Gabriel said. "Water's jes' fine wit' me. I'll jes' watch the horses."

"Okay, Gabriel."

As he entered he saw his men lined up at the bar; they all looked pretty calm. It was Granger who seemed agitated.

". . . just gotta keep your mouth shut, mister. We only came in here for a beer."

"But you brought all them niggers in here with you," the man he was facing said. "Now the place smells."

Ethan approached Ezekial Jackson, who was standing at the end of the bar.

"What's goin' on?"

"Sergeant Granger's just defending the men, Captain," Jackson said. "Some of the folks here aren't too happy about us being here."

"These men are soldiers in the United States Army," Granger told the man.

"Ha!" the man said. "That ain't likely."

He looked to be in his midthirties, and he had a group of men who seemed to be backing him.

"What's the trouble?" Ethan asked, stepping forward.

"This big mouth didn't want the bartender to serve the men, Captain."

Ethan looked at the bar again, saw that none of the men had a drink.

"Well now," he said, "seems to me if we're willin' to pay, the men ought to be able to have a beer."

"Not in here!" the big mouth said.

"Why not?" Ethan asked.

"Because they're niggers!" the man snapped.

"Like my sergeant here told you, they're soldiers in the army."

"And you're their captain?" the man asked.

"That's right."

"Well, you know, the war ain't been over so long that we forgot whose fault it was," the man said.

"Did you fight in the war, mister?" Ethan asked.

"I did."

"Then it seems to me we ought to have a drink together rather than arguin'."

"I ain't havin' no drink with no niggers," the man said, "or with no nigger lovers. You better get your men out of here."

"Mister," Ethan said, "my friend's right. You've got a big mouth. And you must be kinda touched to not notice how outnumbered you are."

The man looked around. He had three or four men behind him, but the rest of the customers in the saloon had backed away.

"I got the whole town behind me!" he snapped, nervously.

"I doubt that," Ethan said. "Now look here, let's

simplify the matter. One of you against one of us. Your man wins, we'll leave. My man wins, we get a beer and then we'll leave."

"We ain't no gunmen," the man said.

"What's your name, friend?" Ethan asked.

"They call me Calico."

"Well, Mr. Calico, we're not gunmen, either, we're soldiers," Ethan said. "I'm not talkin' about a gunfight. I'm just talking hand-to-hand."

"Just fists?" Calico asked.

"That's right."

Calico laughed.

"Mister, you done bit off more than you can chew," Calico said. He turned to his friends. "Go in the back room and get Moose."

"Right," one man said, and ran to the back. He went through a curtained doorway, and when he reappeared he was followed by a man who looked like a walking mountain.

"What's wrong, Calico?" the man asked.

"Moose, these niggers wanna pit one of theirs against one of us in a fistfight. You game?"

Moose cracked his knuckles.

"I'm always ready for a fight, Calico, you know that," Moose said.

While Moose dwarfed the men around him, he seemed to be about ten years younger than them, in his twenties.

"Moose," Ethan said, "why don't you let Calico fight his own battles?"

"Calico's my friend, mister," Moose said. "You the feller I got to fight?"

"No, not me," Ethan said.

"Me," Granger said, stepping forward, but Ethan put his arm out. "No, not you, either, Grange."

"Naw, naw," Calico said, "it's got to be one of the niggers."

Ethan turned and said, "Ezekial?"

The big Black sergeant stepped forward, but he too was dwarfed by Moose.

"I can do it, Captain," he said.

"No, not you, Ezekial," Ethan said. "Why don't you ask your cousin to step in here?"

"Why sure, Captain," Ezekial said. "Noah!"

Jackson's smaller cousin stepped forward.

"Ha!" Calico said. "That's your cousin?"

"He is," Jackson said, "but he isn't going to fight you. Noah, go outside and ask cousin Gabriel to come in."

"Yes, suh!" Noah said, happily.

He ran through the batwing doors, and when he returned, Gabriel was right behind him. There was a sharp intake of breath from the spectators, all of whom were dwarfed by the huge Black man.

"You want me, Captain?" Gabriel asked.

Moose was sizing Gabriel up and down, while Calico simply stared at him with wide eyes.

"I do, Gabriel," Ethan said. "This large gentleman wants to fight one of us, and I don't think any of us wanna fight him. That is, unless you wanna step up."

"Why's he wanna fight, Cap'n?"

"Seems he don't want any of us drinkin' in this saloon," Ethan said.

"Do he own the saloon?" Gabriel asked.

"No, sir, he don't."

"Well then," Gabriel said, "I guess I'm the one's gots to fight, Cap'n."

Moose started to step forward, but Calico stopped him, and pushed him back.

"You sure you wanna do this, Moose?" he asked. "He's pretty big."

"You ever seen anybody beat me, Calico?" Moose asked.

"No, I ain't."

"Then step aside, and let's get this done."

Calico turned to Ethan.

"You heard the man."

# CHAPTER TWENTY-NINE

As the two men faced each other Ethan was hard-pressed to say which was larger. Patrons who had left their tables to stand close to the walls to be out of the line of fire now formed a circle around Gabriel and Moose. Half the circle were townspeople, and the other half were Buffalo Soldiers.

"Any rules?" Calico asked Ethan.

Ethan looked at Ezekial Jackson, who shook his head.

"No rules," Ethan said.

"No bitin'," Moose said. "I hate bitin'. It don't belong in a fight."

"No bitin'?" Calico asked.

"No bitin'," Ethan agreed.

"One more thing, gents!" the bartender called out.

"What's that?" Ethan asked.

"Loser pays the damages."

Ethan and Calico looked at each other, and both said, "Agreed."

"Then make room!" the bartender shouted.

Those forming the circle moved back to widen the space the two big men were occupying. Ethan looked around and saw money changing hands. He looked at Granger, who nodded and moved into the crowd.

"Fight!" Calico shouted.

Gabriel was large and muscular, while Moose was huge and thick. Both men removed their shirts. Gabriel's black skin gleamed, while Moose's upper body was covered with black hair.

The two men began to circle each other. Ethan knew Gabriel was a bare-knuckle champ, but he had the feeling Moose would be more of a wrestler. Sure enough, Moose spread his arms and jumped at Gabriel, trying to envelope him in a bear hug. Gabriel danced aside and Moose staggered by. A cry went up from the crowd, and more money changed hands.

Ethan felt somebody move in behind him, turned, and saw Granger, who nodded.

Moose regained his footing, turned and rushed Gabriel again. Gabriel met him with a right-handed punch which landed on Moose's jaw and staggered him, but the big man shook it off. As he did droplets of blood went flying into the crowd. He wiped his face with one hand, then looked at the blood on his fingertips. It seemed to enrage him.

Gabriel kept his fists up in front of him, his weight equally distributed so that he had a solid base. As Moose came for him again he met him, this time with a push. Moose staggered back, but immediately came forward again. As he grabbed for Gabriel, the big Black man ducked and threw a punch that struck Moose in the ribs. Ethan thought he could feel the vibrations of the punch beneath his feet.

Moose bent over, holding his side, but straightened and charged again. Ethan thought Gabriel was going to have to hit the big man more than once, each time, or he'd just keep shaking it off and coming.

As if reading Ethan's mind, Gabriel met Moose's next charge with a right and a left. Blood flew from Moose's face, from his nose and from a cut under one eye.

Ethan had the feeling this was going to be too easy for Gabriel, but then Moose changed his tactic. The next time he charged he stopped short and threw a punch of his own. His massive fist made contact with Gabriel's jaw, which made the Black man blink several times.

Moose threw another punch, which Gabriel ducked. He then punched Moose quickly in the ribs three times—rat-tat-tat—causing Moose to stagger back. Instead of waiting for the big man to charge again, Gabriel moved in after him. He hit him in the face again, a right, a left, and a right. Moose was stunned. But as Gabriel went to throw another punch. Moose looked as if he was falling forward. Gabriel held the punch back, and Moose abruptly spread his arms and finally caught Gabriel in a massive bear hug.

Moose roared, feeling his moment of triumph was at hand. He squeezed and actually lifted Gabriel off his feet as he tried to hug the air out of him.

Gabriel's expression never changed. He didn't look concerned. He seemed to swell, as he tried to break the big white man's hold. Finally, he slammed his forehead into Moose's. Blood spewed, and for a moment it wasn't clear whose blood it was, but then Moose released Gabriel and staggered back. Suddenly, a curtain of blood came from his lacerated forehead and fell into his eyes. He couldn't see, and Gabriel took advantage of that. He stepped in and threw punches—one, two, three, four—drew his fist back for another as Moose suddenly fell forward onto his face.

It got very quiet as Gabriel looked down at the fallen man. Turning, he walked over to Ethan.

"Okay, Gabriel," he said, "have a drink."

"I don't drink, Cap'n."

"Oh, that's right," Ethan said. He looked at the bartender. "Give him some water."

"Yes, sir."

Calico and his friends leaned over the fallen Moose, who still hadn't moved.

"I think he killed 'im," Calico said, staring up at Ethan.

"I doubt it," Ethan said. He looked at the bartender. "Let me have some water, too."

The barman handed him a glass.

"Turn 'im over," Ethan said.

Calico turned Moose onto his back, and Ethan dumped the glass of water in the fallen man's face. Moose came to, immediately sputtering.

"Now if you don't mind," Ethan said to Calico, "my men are gonna have their drinks."

Calico scowled. He and his friends helped Moose to his feet and to the back room.

Ethan joined Granger at the bar while the bartender began setting the Buffalo Soldiers up with beers. He put a mug in front of the two white men, as well.

"Did you collect on your bets?" Ethan asked.

"I did," Granger said. "We did real well, since everybody was backin' that big fella."

The Buffalo Soldiers were happily drinking their beer and slapping Gabriel on the back.

"What should I do with the money, Ethan?" Granger asked.

"Buy some provisions before we leave town. Get bacon to go with the beans, and more coffee."

"Right."

"Take Gabriel with you, and buy him somethin'," Ethan said.

"Okay."

Granger went over to Gabriel, got him to put his shirt back on, and then walked out with him.

"What'd I tell you, Captain?" Sergeant Ezekial Jackson said, coming over to stand next to Ethan. "Undefeated."

"Yeah, you told me, all right."

"Did you get any information from the sheriff?" Jackson asked.

"I did," Ethan said. "I'll tell you and Granger about it later. Have the men drink up. As soon as Granger and Gabriel are done at the mercantile, we'll ride out."

"Yes, sir."

Ethan looked at the bartender as Jackson walked away.

"No damages, right?" he said.

"No damages," the bartender agreed. "That was really somethin'. I ain't never seen Moose lose a fight."

"There's always a first time."

"If I was you," the bartender said, "I'd get outta town fast."

"Why's that?"

"He wasn't wearin' his badge," the bartender said, "but Moose is a deputy. Your man knocked out a lawman."

"It was a fair fight."

"You'd have to tell that to the sheriff."

Ethan shook his head.

SERGEANT JACKSON GOT the Buffalo Soldiers mounted, and Ethan doled out the supplies he and Gabriel bought so that each man was carrying something rather than having it all on one horse.

As Ethan was about to mount his horse he saw the sheriff crossing the street toward him.

"Trouble?" Granger asked.

"I don't know," Ethan said. He went to meet the man.

"I thought I asked you to try not to cause any trouble," Sheriff Colby said.

"I did, Sheriff."

"Your man whipped my deputy," Colby said, "a man who had never been whipped before."

"I thought that was better than havin' a brawl," Ethan said. "One man against one, to settle the matter."

"I could put your man in my jail, you know."

"I'd prefer you didn't, Sheriff," Ethan said, "because then I couldn't guarantee there'd be no trouble."

Colby looked up at the mounted Buffalo Soldiers, and then back at Ethan.

"Don't come back here," he said to Ethan.

"I don't see any reason we'd have to, Sheriff," Ethan said.

He mounted his horse, and led the Buffalo Soldiers out of Sheffield.


OUTSIDE OF TOWN Ethan stopped and spoke with Granger and Jackson.

"Valverde?" Granger asked.

"That's what the sheriff said," Ethan answered.

"Was he on the level, Ethan?"

"I don't see why not," Ethan said.

"Wasn't there a Battle of Valverde?" Jackson asked.

"Yeah," Granger said, "one of the few Confederate victories in Texas."

"I guess that would make sense, then," Jackson said. "A fitting place for Ashforth to put his headquarters if he's looking to start the war, again."

"When we camp tonight," Ethan said to Jackson, "let the men know where we'll be goin', and why."

"Yes, sir."

"How's Gabriel doin'?"

"He's got one or two bruises, but otherwise he's fine," Jackson said.

"Good," Ethan said, "Ezekial, you and Noah take the point."

"Yes, sir."

Jackson rode ahead with his cousin, which left Ethan and Granger alone, side-by-side.

"Did you buy Gabriel somethin' he wanted?" Ethan asked.

"I did."

"What was it?"

"He just wanted some hard candy," Granger said. "I got him a bag."

"That was some fight," Ethan said, as they rode along.

"Poor Moose," Granger said. "He's gonna be sore for a while. What was the sheriff's beef?"

"That fella Moose was his deputy," Ethan said.

"Wha—" Granger was totally surprised. "He wasn't wearin' no badge."

"I know," Ethan said.

"Did he wanna lock Gabriel up?"

"He mentioned it," Ethan said. "I managed to talk him out of it."

"Jesus," Granger said with a laugh, "we would've had to break him out."

"I know," Ethan said. "I indicated as much to the sheriff. He then preferred that we just ride out and never come back."

"Suits me," Granger said.

"Me, too."

# CHAPTER THIRTY

They bypassed the town of Ozuna and camped for the night. Noah used the new provisions to prepare bacon and beans, and also did some chuck wagon biscuits in another pan Granger had purchased. With Moze and Abraham back at the fort, they weren't going to be eating as well as they had on the drive.

They built two fires close together so, basically, the twenty-two men could sit around and eat together. That way Ethan felt he could fill them in on where they were going, instead of having Jackson do it.

"So we're headin' for Valverde," Ethan finished, "in the hopes that Ashforth is camped somewhere near there, with the weapons."

"Are we gonna ride right in, bold as you please?" a man named Samson asked.

"No, we can't do that," Ethan said. "We'd attract too much attention. No, I think Granger and me will ride in, while the rest of you camp outside of town. We might take one more man with us, so we can send him back to get the rest of you if it comes to that."

"What if they're camped north of Valverde," Jackson said, "and we ride smack dab into them?"

"That's a good point," Ethan said. "Kerrville is just north of Valverde. Maybe when we get that far, we'll send Noah on ahead to scout."

"We'll come to Sonora before that," Granger said. "It might be a good idea to talk to the law there, see what they know. I mean, that seems to have worked with Sheffield—except for the fight, it went well."

"The fight went good, too," Noah said, and they all laughed.

"How are you feelin', Gabriel?" Granger asked. "Any ailments durin' the ride here?"

"No, sir," Gabriel said. "I be fine. It was probably the shortest fight I ever had. I gone twenty, thirty rounds in the past."

"I thought that fella Moose was gonna be more trouble," Granger said.

"He was more of a wrestler than a fighter," Ethan said.

"He was strong," Gabriel said. "I got lucky."

"I don't think luck had anythin' to do with it, big fella," Granger said. "Those last four punches were things of beauty." Granger raised his plate. "And we're eatin' thanks to our winnin's."

"Anybody else make any bets?" Ethan asked.

All the Black men looked around at each other, and then Samson said, "We ain't had any money ta bet with, suh."

"Well," Ethan said "it was a last-minute idea. I saw money changing hands and it sorta made me mad to have all those people bettin' against you, Gabriel."

"That's fine with me, suh," Gabriel said. "I's happy with the bacon and biscuits bein' added to the beans."

"So are we all," Ethan said.

They finished eating and then prepared to turn in for the night. Granger and Jackson decided on who would be standing watch, and which soldiers would be relieving who.

"One more thing!" Ethan called out, as the men began to leave the fires. "If any of you don't want to go to Valverde for any reason, I'll understand. You can stay behind."

They all looked around at each other and then Ezekial Jackson spoke up.

"Captain, we'd be deserters if we did that."

"I wouldn't be reportin' anyone," Ethan said. "You could stay right here and wait for us to pick you up on the way back. Nobody at Fort Davis needs to know anythin' about it."

The Buffalo Soldiers exchanged glances again, and then Jackson said, "If it's all the same, Captain, we'll just stay with you."

The men all nodded.

"Well, that suits me fine," Ethan said. "Get some rest."


WHEN ALL THE men were asleep except for the two on watch, Ethan and Granger sat at a fire and drank coffee.

"When we get to Sonora," Ethan said, "let's not all ride in. I don't want a replay of what happened in Sheffield."

"I think the men will understand that."

"You and me can ride in and talk to the sheriff," Ethan said, "then ride right back out, again."

"That suits me," Granger said.

They continued to drink coffee until the big iron pot was empty, and then Granger made a fresh pot.

"I meant to ask," Granger said, "do we have any idea how many men Ashforth has? A dozen? fifty? More?"

"As a matter of fact," Ethan said, "we don't. But if he's lookin' to start another war, I'd think it was more like fifty than a dozen."

"If there was a telegraph in Fort Davis and we could locate Ashforth's camp, then we'd be able to notify them."

"When Fort Davis was first built there was no thought of a telegraph," Ethan said. "If they tried to string one now, it would take forever."

"And Stockton?"

"All these forts from the Rio Grande to the Concho were closed for a long time, and have only recently been rebuilt and occupied. The best we'd be able to do is send a telegram to Sheffield, or El Paso, and then hope somebody rides out to the fort with it. And we can't depend on that."

"So it's just us," Granger said.

"That was the idea when Merritt decided to send the Buffalo Soldiers, Grange."

Granger looked around the camp at the sleeping men. The two on watch were sitting at the other fire, and exchanged a nod with him.

"I'm guessing these men can fight," Granger said, "but we won't find out until the time comes."

"Wasn't it the same in the war, whenever we got new recruits?" Ethan said. "Baptism by fire."

"John the Baptist, Matthew three-eleven," Granger quoted.

Ethan stared at him.

"I've known you all these years and you ain't never quoted the Bible to me."

"Ya learn somethin' new every day, don't ya?" Granger said, with a smile.

\* \* \*

I N THE MORNING Noah rose early and made more biscuits for breakfast. They all washed them down with
coffee, and then got underway. As they rode Ethan
explained to Jackson what he and Granger had discussed, about keeping the men out of town, this time.

"I agree," Jackson said.

"I don't want the men to feel . . . insulted."

"You're the captain," Jackson reminded him. "They'll
go along with whatever you decide."

"Yeah, they will," Ethan said, "as long as you will. I
know the men respect you, Ezekial."

"And you, Captain," Jackson said. "You just tell us
what you want us to do, and we'll keep doing it."

Jackson rode ahead to travel alongside Noah.
Granger came over to ride alongside Ethan.

"What about those two Comanches?" Ethan asked.
"After Sheffield I pretty much forgot about them when
I started concentrating on Ashforth."

"I ain't seen 'em," Granger said, "and neither has
Noah. Of course, that don't mean they ain't there."

"Maybe they've moved on, lookin' for easier prey,"
Ethan suggested.

"Hopefully."

They didn't know how prophetic their words would
be . . .

T HEY WERE JUST outside of Sonora when they heard
shots in the distance.

"They're coming from there?" Jackson pointed north.

"Sonora's that way," Granger said, pointing south.

"Damn it!" Ethan said. "Let's take a look."

They all headed north at a gallop.

As they rode the shots became louder and louder,

until they saw the activity up ahead. Two wagons were being surrounded by what looked like Comanches.

"They're outnumbered," Granger said. "Even though the Indians only have bows."

"I hear shots," Ethan said, "but I don't see any bodies. We'd better give them a hand." If they had a bugler Ethan would have had him blow, but he drew his pistol and shouted, "Charge!"

They drew their guns and galloped toward the action. Ethan started firing, but it was only for show—they were too far to be effective—and the others followed.

The Comanches turned and saw the men riding toward them. Ethan knew they must have been confused, not seeing any uniforms on a group of Black men charging at them.

A few of the Buffalo Soldiers put their rifles to work, and this time their shots were effective. Several Comanches fell from their horses. The others decided to run and fight another day.

"Jackson!" Ethan shouted. "Don't let the men chase them!"

"Yessir."

Jackson quickly rode ahead, then turned his horse and waved the men off. Ethan changed direction and rode toward the two wagons. Several people stepped out from behind them, rifles still in hand.

Ethan knew the Buffalo Soldiers must have presented an odd image, but he and Granger were in front. Seeing two white men, the rifles' barrels were lowered to point to the ground as they approached.

"Are you all right?" Ethan called. "Any injuries?"

"A couple," a man said.

"Serious?" Ethan asked.

"We don't know." The spokesman looked behind Ethan at the approaching Black men. "We owe you our lives, but . . . who are you?"

"Soldiers from Fort Davis," Ethan said, dismounting.

"Black soldiers?" a woman asked. She moved next to the man who was speaking, and took his arm. They were middle-aged, and probably married.

"They're called Buffalo Soldiers," Ethan said.

"But . . . no uniforms?" the man asked.

"We're on a special assignment," Ethan said. "I'm Captain Miller, this is Sergeant Granger, and that's Sergeant Jackson." Ethan turned to Ezekial. "Sergeant, keep the men on watch from every direction. They might be reforming for another attack."

"Yes, sir."

The woman's hold on her husband's arm tightened.

"Do you really think they'll come back?" she asked.

"Not while we're here," Ethan said, "but it never hurts to be careful. Can we look at your wounded?"

"Yes," the man said, "this way."

As they walked Ethan said, "We heard the shots, but didn't see any dead Comanches."

"We're farmers," the man said. "We're not very good shots."

"Farmers?"

"On our way west to make a new home," the man said.

"You have children with you?" Ethan asked.

Before the man could answer two young girls and a small boy came running over to the couple, who gathered them into their arms.

"We do," the man said.

# CHAPTER THIRTY-ONE

IT TURNED OUT there were three families traveling in the two wagons—six adults and eight children. The six adults were three married couples, two were in their thirties and the couple Ethan had met were in their forties. They were all part of the same family, whose last name was Avery. William and Alice Avery were pretty much considered the leaders.

The two wounded were one man and one woman, from each of the other couples. The man had an arrow in his thigh, while the woman was struck on her right shoulder.

One of the Buffalo Soldiers had worked in a medical tent during the war, so he and Granger examined the wounded.

"Dey not bad, Sarge," Christian said to Granger.

"Good," Granger said. "I'll look at the man and tell the family."

"Now you's bite down, missy, while I take this arrow

out," Christian said to the woman, whose eyes were wide with fright. "you's gon' be all right."

Granger didn't know if she was afraid of her wound, or of the Black man working on her. But he had no time to reassure the woman. His attention was on the man in front of him.

"You'll be fine, mister. We gotta get that arrow out. You just sit tight."

The man nodded.

Granger walked to where Ethan stood with William and Alice Avery.

"How are my brother and sister-in-law?" William asked.

"They're gonna be fine," Granger said, then looked at the woman. "Ma'am, if I was you I'd go and sit with the lady. She's pretty scared."

"Yes, of course," Alice said.

As she started away the children tried to follow.

"Don't take the kids," Granger said. "It's gonna be kinda bloody."

"Children," William called out, "you stay here with daddy."

The children turned and came back.

"You're headed west, Mr. Avery," Ethan said. "You're bound to run into more Indians. I suggest you go to Sonora. That's where we're headed."

"Is there farmland there?" Avery asked.

"Probably not—"

"We're farmers, Captain," Avery said. "We're headin' for California."

Ethan looked at the man's rifle, which was pretty old.

"Then if I was you, first chance I got I'd buy better weapons and learn how to shoot them," he advised.

"Perhaps you could teach us," the man said, "before you ride on? Just a lesson or two, to improve our chances?"

Ethan knew it would take more than a few lessons to improve their chances against the Comanches.

"I tell you what," Ethan said. "Let's get you moved to a different location, camped, and then we'll see what we can do."

THEY GOT THE two wounded people looked after, and loaded onto a wagon each. Then they got all the children loaded. Finally, they got the wagons moving, surrounded by the Buffalo Soldiers in case of another attack. But the Indians didn't return.

They moved on for a few hours, Ethan directing the wagons southwest, so that he and the Buffalo Soldiers were not going back the way they came so far. They were still pretty much moving close to Sonora.

Finally, he chose a place to camp. They unloaded the wounded and children from the wagons, then formed a picket line for the horses. They built three fires and both Noah and the women of the Avery family began to cook.

Ethan sat with Granger, Jackson, and William Avery.

"If we're gonna give you shootin' lessons," he said, "it's gonna hafta be all of you."

"The women, too?"

"If you encounter Indians again, you'll need as many people firing weapons as possible. That means even the older children. The Comanches were able to tell that only a few of you were firing. They were playin' with you when we came along because they knew they could take you anytime they wanted."

"My God," the man said, "and I thought we were holding them off."

"Not at all," Granger said. "They had you at their mercy."

"I'm certainly glad we didn't know that at the time," Avery said.

"Well, you know it, now," Granger said. "You get your women and the older children together with you and your brothers, and we'll get started."

"We don't have weapons for everyone," William said. "It never occurred to me that I would have to arm my children."

Ethan looked at Jackson.

"Do we have any extra weapons?" he asked.

"Maybe a few," Jackson said. "I have an extra pistol in my saddlebag, but—"

"I know," Ethan said, "they need rifles, but at least a pistol will make some noise. See what else you can find."

"Yes, sir."

Jackson went off to find extra weapons, though Ethan was sure he and his men could hardly afford to give them away.

"Ethan," Granger said.

"Yeah?"

"Christian gave me this," Granger said, showing Ethan an arrow. "It's the one he took out of the man's thigh."

Ethan accepted it.

"What does it tell us?" he asked.

"That these Indians weren't Comanches."

"Then what tribe were they?"

"Lipan Apaches," Granger said. "They come up from Mexico to raid."

"What's the difference, Grange?" Ethan asked.

"Not much really," Granger said. "Comanches and Apaches are both deadly warriors. But they don't much get along with each other."

"Well then, it's too bad we don't have a band of Comanches to pit against them, so they'd leave these people alone. No matter what we teach 'em when we leave them, they'll be dead within ten miles."

"We could send some men with them," Granger said. "Say, six of the Buffalo Soldiers? Just to see them as far as, maybe Sheffield?"

"That's too far back the way we came," Ethan said. "We need all the men we have, Grange."

"Then what do we do?" Granger asked.

"Teach them what you can," Ethan said, "and meanwhile, I'll try to talk Avery into lettin' us escort them to Sonora. A doctor could look after their wounded, they could buy some new weapons, and maybe hire an escort."

"Or they could wait for us to come back, and we could escort them through Texas, at least as far as Fort Davis."

Ethan studied Granger for a moment, and the man knew what he was thinking.

"I know," he said, "there's no guarantee we'll be comin' back."

"It's still a good idea, though," Ethan said. "It might convince them to stay put in Sonora for a while."

"Sonora's no place for farmers."

"Neither is the Texas prairie, without some sort of escort," Ethan added. "I'm just tryin' to keep these children alive as long as possible."

"Chances are the Apaches would take the children," Granger said, "after they kill the adults."

Ethan brightened.

"That's good stuff, Grange," he said. "Make sure you tell 'em that."

"You wanna scare 'em into stayin' in Sonora?"

"Damn right!" Ethan said.


ETHAN WATCHED AS Granger and a few of the Buffalo Soldiers instructed the family—men, women *and* children—how to shoot. Jackson had managed to scrounge up an extra pistol, two extra rifles, and a shotgun. At one point, he found himself standing next to William Avery, watching.

"All these years I thought all there was to shooting a rifle was to point it and pull the trigger," Avery said.

"The point is," Ethan said, "to fire the rifle effectively. To be effective, you have to hit what you're aimin' at."

"Yes, Sergeant Granger explained that to me," Avery said. "Aim and squeeze, don't jerk the trigger. And lead your target. There's so much to remember. I hope the children can do it."

"Like I said," Ethan replied, "you just need to have as many people firing weapons as possible, to convince the Indians that you're all dangerous."

"Sergeant Granger also told me the Indians were Apaches," Avery said.

"Apaches or Comanches," Ethan said, "they're all dangerous."

"May I ask you something, Captain?" Avery said.

"Go ahead."

"Granger seems to be of the opinion that my family and I will be killed as soon as we part company with you," Avery said. "Do you share that opinion?"

"I'm afraid I do, Mr. Avery," Ethan said.

"He also seems to think we should stay in Sonora and wait for you and your soldiers to return," Avery said. "He said then you would be able to escort us safely to someplace called Fort Davis?"

"That's where we came from," Ethan said.

"Well . . . just how long would we have to be in Sonora?" Avery asked. "I mean, how long would it be before you return?"

Here was the tricky part. He didn't want to tell Avery they might never return. If they were all killed, he wanted Avery to have to deal with it when the time came.

"I can't say for sure, Mr. Avery," Ethan said. "But I'm sure you and your family could put the time to good use. For one thing, your wounded would have time to heal. And you and your brothers might be able to earn some money with odd jobs, and buy yourself some new weapons. Also, your teams would get some rest, and so would your children. Finally, you'd all be able to recover emotionally from the attack."

"You certainly make it sound logical for us to stay," Avery said.

"I believe it is logical," Ethan said.

"I'd have to talk with my family about it."

"You do that," Ethan said. "You don't have to decide anythin' until mornin'."

"Thank you for all your help, Captain," Avery said, and went to join his family.

LATER, ETHAN ASKED Granger, "What d'ya think?"
"I think what you think," Granger said. "They're dead if they don't stop in Sonora."

They both looked over at the Avery family, huddled together around one fire.

"Those are nice kids," Granger said. "I just hope the family doesn't continue to be stubborn, and get them killed."

# CHAPTER THIRTY-TWO

ETHAN SET A watch, in case the Apaches decided to come back. He heard several of the children cry out during the night, as if having nightmares, and didn't blame them. Not after what they had been through. He hoped the bad dreams would help William Avery and his family come to the right decision. If they didn't, then Ethan felt he might have to put his foot down and force the family to go to Sonora. He couldn't, in all good conscience, allow the family to move on and get killed. Once he got them to Sonora, and he and his men continued on to Valverde, they could do what they wanted, and he wouldn't feel guilty about it.

In the morning, as they had breakfast, Granger explained he had come to the same conclusion.

"If they don't make the right decision, Ethan, we're gonna hafta force them."

"Agreed," Ethan said. "I spent the night thinkin' exactly the same thing."

"Good," Granger said, with relief. "If they wanna

go and get themselves killed after we leave them in Sonora, that's their decision. We'll be too busy to worry about them."

While the Buffalo Soldiers saddled their horses, Ethan and Granger went to William Avery.

"I told my family everything we talked about," Avery said, "and we've all agreed . . ."

Ethan and Granger both held their breath.

". . . to go to Sonora with you. We feel it at least makes sense to give our wounded time to heal."

"That's great!" Granger said, excited by their decision.

Avery looked at him with a surprised expression.

"We were worried you were gonna insist on continuing west," Ethan said. "If you had, you'd all be dead within a day."

"You're makin' the right decision," Granger assured the man.

Avery went to get his family and their two wagons ready. He and his brother hitched up their teams. When Ethan heard the laughter of the children he looked over and found them playing with Gabriel. The big man had several of them up on his broad shoulders, while others clung to his tree trunk legs. Gabriel was laughing loudly with them, like a big kid, himself. He carried them to their wagons and lifted them up inside.

When all the men were mounted and the families in their wagons, they started for Sonora.

ETHAN SENT THREE soldiers ahead to scout for the Apaches, in case the Indians decided to get between them and Sonora. It didn't happen, and by late afternoon they were approaching the town.

Ethan called a halt to their progress, and the Buffalo Soldiers dismounted.

"What's happening?" William Avery asked.

"My men will camp here," Ethan said. "Sergeant Granger and me will ride into Sonora with you, and get you settled."

"But why must your men stay out here?" Alice Avery asked.

"Mrs. Avery, there are still people in South Texas who are holdin' on to the war. They wouldn't be happy to see twenty Black men ridin' into their town."

"Is that the kind of place you're suggesting we spend time in?" she asked.

"Not at all," Ethan said. "I'm not even sure they'd feel that way, but I'm tryin' to avoid any trouble."

Avery put his hand on his wife's arm and said, "The captain knows what he's doing, dear."

She fell silent, but was still not pleased.

Ethan gave Sergeant Jackson his orders to settle in for the night and keep on the lookout for the Apaches.

"Granger and me, we'll be back here for supper," Ethan said.

"You're not going to stay in town?" Jackson asked.

"No," Ethan said, "we'll be there long enough to get these folks settled, and to talk to the law about Ashforth. Hopefully, the sheriff will know somethin'."

Ethan, Granger, and the Avery family continued on while the Buffalo Soldiers made camp . . .

S ONORA WAS NOT a large town, so the two wagons driving in attracted attention.

"It seems a rather sleepy place," Alice Avery observed.

"It'll get lively," Ethan told her. "We're only about ninety miles from Mexico. You'll find both American and Mexican culture here."

She put her hand on her husband's arm, and he reached over and patted it to soothe her.

Ethan halted their progress right in front of the sheriff's office.

"I'm gonna go in and talk to the sheriff," he told them. "He might have some idea of where you can settle in for your stay."

People stopped to stare as the children stuck their heads out of their wagons and waved.

Ethan entered the sheriff's office, prepared to show his printed orders to identify himself properly. He found a tall man in his forties, wearing a sheriff's star, cleaning the guns in his gun rack with a rag. He turned as he heard Ethan enter.

"Can I help ya?"

"Sheriff, my name's Ethan Miller. I'm leading a company from Fort Davis. We're looking for Ashforth's Raiders. I was wonderin' if you might've heard anythin' useful?"

The lawman replaced the rifle he was cleaning into the rack, tossed the rag aside, and faced Ethan.

"What've *you* heard?" he asked.

"That he and his men might be headquartered somewhere around Valverde."

"That'd make sense, given Valverde's history," the sheriff said. "But I'm afraid I can't confirm or deny that. Sorry."

"Have they raided in your area recently?"

"That I can answer, because they haven't," the lawman said. "I'd suggest you stop in Kerrville, Mr. Miller. The law there might know more than I do."

"That would be our next logical stop," Ethan agreed. "Well, that brings me to my next problem." He explained to the man about rescuing the Avery family from the Apaches, and bringing them into town.

"There's a clearing on the south end of town where they could put their wagons and camp, if they can't afford a hotel."

"I think a hotel would be beyond their means," Ethan said. "And they've got eight children with them. But if you've got a doctor—"

"We do, and say no more." The man reached for his hat. "I can have the doc come and see them. Just continue on through town until you get to the end of the street and you'll see the clearin' I mean."

"The family is out front, so why I don't introduce you, and we'll go from there."

"That's fine," the man said. "My name's Al Gracy, by the way."

They went outside and Ethan introduced the sheriff to Granger and the Avery family.

"I've told Mr. Miller where you can park your wagons," Sheriff Gracy said. "I'll bring the doc to you so he can tend to your wounded."

"We appreciate that very much, Sheriff," Alice Avery said.

"Yes, much obliged, Sheriff," Avery said.

Ethan and Granger led the two wagons to the clearing, where they stopped. The Averys stepped down and looked around.

"I suppose we'd be safe camped here," Avery said. "The Apaches won't come into town, will they?"

"I doubt it," Granger said. "You were easy pickin's out there. Not so easy here."

"This'll do, then," Avery told Ethan. "We can wait here for you. The children can sleep in the wagons."

"Grange and me'll help you make camp, wait while the doc looks at your brother and your sister-in-law."

"We might as well start by unhitchin' the teams," Granger said.

While they were getting the horses settled the sheriff appeared with another man he introduced as Doc Henry. The doctor was in his sixties, but spry enough to climb into each wagon to examine the wounded. When he came out of the second one he faced Ethan.

"Whoever took those arrows out and cleaned the wounds did a nice job."

"I'll tell him you said so."

"Did he have medical training?"

"Just what he learned in a medical tent during the war," Ethan said.

"That explains it, then," Henry said. "He had experience with wounds." Doc Henry turned to Avery. "I can come back tomorrow and check on them. Meanwhile, they just need some rest. I can even examine the children, if you like."

"Thank you, Doctor. We'd appreciate that very much."

Doc Henry tipped his hat to Alice Avery and left.

E THAN AND GRANGER helped the Averys get settled in. They built a fire and got some coffee going, offered some to the sheriff, who accepted.

"Sheriff, how are the people in town gonna accept the Averys?" Ethan asked.

"Oh, I think they'll be very acceptin'," Sheriff Gracy said. "Many of them were travelers once, lookin' for a place to light. They know what it's like. Most of the people hereabouts are friendly."

"That's good."

"How long do you figure they'll be waitin' here for you?" Gracy asked.

"Between you and me, Sheriff," Ethan said, "there's a chance we might never come back. If we find Ashforth and he's got fifty men or so, we could be in a lot of trouble. If we don't come back, this family will have to make a decision."

"Well," Gracy said, "if they still wanna be farmers, they'll have to move on."

"If and when that happens," Ethan said, "maybe you can arrange some sort of escort."

"Hmm, I'll have to see," Gracy said. "After all, we're talkin' about Apaches, and probably Comanches. To tell you the truth, Mr. Miller, I don't know how this family got this far."

"To tell you the truth, Sheriff," Ethan said, "neither do I."

E THAN AND GRANGER got to the Buffalo Soldier camp in time for supper.

"How's the family doing?" Ezekial Jackson said.

"Them kids all right, Cap'n?" Gabriel asked.

"They're fine," Ethan said. "There'll be a doctor lookin' them kids over tomorrow. Christian, the doctor was impressed by what you did."

"Thank ya, Cap'n," Christian said.

"They going to stay there, Captain?" Jackson asked.

"Ezekial, I think they'll stay awhile. If they're still here when we come back, we can take them with us."

"And if we don't get back?" Jackson asked.

"I'm afraid they'll be on their own," Ethan said.

# CHAPTER THIRTY-THREE

Believing the Avery family to now be safe, Ethan, Granger, and the Buffalo Soldiers continued their ride to Valverde. Their next stop before reaching there would be the town of Kerrville.

"Same deal, Ethan?" Granger asked, as they approached the town limits. "You and me go in, the Buffalo Soldiers make camp?"

"Yeah, I think so, Grange," Ethan said. "I'm still lookin' to avoid trouble, but I also don't want word to get around that there are twenty Black men ridin' in the area."

"You're afraid word'll get to Ashforth?"

Ethan nodded.

"Would that be such a bad thing?" Granger asked.

Ethan stared at Granger for a moment, thinking about that question.

"Maybe not," he said, finally. "You're thinkin' it might bring him out into the open?"

Granger nodded.

"That's what I'm thinkin'."

Ethan looked around at the Buffalo Soldiers.

"How do you think these fellas will like bein' hung out as bait?" he asked.

"Well," Granger said, "you could ask 'em, or you could tell 'em."

Ethan located Jackson and rode up alongside him.

"Change of plans, Sergeant," he said. "We're all gonna ride into Kerrville, bold as you please."

"Why the change?"

"We want word to get to Ashforth," Ethan said.

"Being who he is," Jackson said, "he won't be able to resist comin' after us."

"And we'll be waitin' for him."

"But where?"

"That's what we're gonna figure out," Ethan said, "over cold beers in the nearest saloon."


T HE TWENTY-TWO MEN rode into Kerrville and attracted a lot of attention, which was the point.
They stopped at the first saloon they saw, The Outlaw.

It was midday, so there was plenty of room for all twenty-two men at the bar, and at tables. The locals who were there chose to put their drinks down and leave.

"What the hell do ya think you're doin'?" the bartender demanded.

"I'm buyin' beer for all my men," Ethan said.

"You can't just take over The Outlaw," the man said.

"We're not."

"You drove my customers out!" the man accused.

"Hey," Ethan said, "we didn't ask 'em to leave. Now, I need twenty-two cold beers."

The bartender stared at him, then said, "Comin' up."

They were all having beers when the batwing doors

opened and a tall man in his thirties, wearing a marshal's badge, came in.

"I'm Marshal Ed Drover," he said. "Who's in charge here?"

"I am," Ethan said. "Captain Ethan Miller, US Cavalry."

"Can you prove that?"

Ethan took his orders out of his shirt and handed them over.

"This says you're lookin' for missin' weapons," Drover said, handing them back.

"That's right."

"And these are your soldiers?"

"Buffalo Soldiers, like it says here," Ethan said, stuffing the orders back into his shirt.

"Why are you out of uniform?"

"It was Colonel Merritt's idea, out of Fort Davis. He thought the Comanches might leave us alone if they didn't see uniforms, or white faces," Ethan said, giving Merritt credit for his idea.

"I see two white faces," Drover said.

"And twenty Black ones," Ethan said. "So far it seems to be workin'."

Drover looked around at all the Black men drinking beer and looking back at him.

"How about a beer, Marshal?" Ethan asked. "On the cavalry?"

"Why not?" Drover said. He looked at the bartender. "Gimme one, Sam."

"You gonna let all these niggers take over my place, Marshal?" the bartender demanded, handing Drover his beer.

"Why don't you watch your mouth, Sam?" Drover suggested. "Captain Miller, can we sit?"

"Sure, why not? Grange," he called. "Marshal, this is Sergeant Granger."

"Glad to meet you," Drover said.

The three men walked to an empty table in the back of the room.

"Where are you headed, Captain?" Drover asked.

"Valverde."

"Why there?"

"We heard Ashforth's Raiders might be headquartered there."

"And you think they stole your weapons? Not the Comanches, or Apaches?"

"Have you heard of any Indians' raid bein' made with rifles?" Ethan asked.

"Nope, can't say I have."

"How about Ashforth?" Ethan said. "Any word about him in the area?"

"He ain't been raidin' around here," Drover said, "but I gotta admit I heard the same thing you did about Valverde."

"That's good," Ethan said. "I'd hate to think we were chasin' our own tail. What else can you tell me? Any idea of how many men he has?"

"Not really," Drover said. "But some men came to town a few weeks ago with two buckboards and bought a bunch of supplies from the mercantile."

"You think they were Ashforth's men?"

"I didn't at the time," Drover said, "but I do now."

Ethan looked at Granger.

"If we find out what they bought, it might give us some idea how many men we're dealin' with."

"You gonna send for help?" Drover asked. "Or try to handle 'em yourselves?"

"I think we're gonna handle it ourselves."

"And how do you intend to do that?" Drover asked.

"That's not somethin' I can talk about, Marshal," Ethan said. "We don't want our tactics to get around."

"Who do you think I'd tell?"

"I don't know," Ethan said. "Maybe nobody. I'm just playin' it safe, Marshal."

Drover looked around, then back at Ethan.

"This doesn't look like what I'd call playin' it safe," he said. "Word's gonna get around."

"I figured it would."

"Aw, now wait a minute," Drover said. "You and your men ain't gonna wait here for Ashforth and his men to come ridin' in. I ain't havin' that kinda shoot-out on my streets."

"I'm not lookin' for that, Marshal," Ethan said. "I wouldn't want any innocent to get hurt. We'll be ridin' out."

"I'm glad to hear it," Marshal Drover said. "When?"

"Don't worry," Ethan said. "Before the end of the day."

Drover stood up.

"I guess that suits me, Captain," Drover said. "I wish you and your men luck."

"Thanks," Ethan said.

Drover started for the door, then stopped.

"There's an abandoned rock quarry just south of town," he said. "It would offer a lot of cover for a lot of men. You might take a look. You won't be able to miss it. You'll have to pass it on the way to Valverde, and so will anybody comin' the other way."

"Much obliged, Marshal," Ethan said.

Drover left the saloon, ignoring the bartender's anxious waves.

Ethan walked to the bar. The man stopped waving and looked at him.

"One more beer each," Ethan said, "and then we'll be on our way."

"Yeah, yeah," the bartender said, and he started

setting them up. Ethan grabbed three and went back to his table, where Granger was waiting. He waved Jackson over.

"The marshal says there's a rock quarry not far from here that might make a good place to stand off Ashforth and his raiders."

"If they come," Jackson said.

"That's right," Ethan said, "if they come. We might have to wait some time for word to reach them, but I'm thinkin' it might not be that long."

"The marshal?" Granger asked. "You figure he'll be the one to tell Ashforth about us?"

"I don't think so," Ethan said, "but I do think somebody from town will get the word to him."

"What makes you think so?" Jackson asked.

"Ashforth's not stupid," Ethan said. "He'd have people placed strategically to gather information for him."

"So how long do we wait?" Jackson asked.

"As long as it takes," Ethan said. "We'll ride to that rock quarry and have a look. Meanwhile, pick two men out to ride on ahead. If they see him they're to ride back and let us know. Tell them not to engage."

"They won't, Captain," Jackson said. "I guarantee it."

Jackson went to talk to the men.

"You think the marshal's tryin' to be helpful?" Granger asked. "He could be lurin' us into a trap."

"There's no harm in takin' a look," Ethan said.

"I thought we'd just stay here, in Kerrville," Granger offered.

"I don't want any innocent people gettin' killed, Grange," Ethan said. "And the army wouldn't appreciate it, either."

"You're the boss, Ethan," Granger said.

"Hey, this was your idea."

"Don't remind me," Granger said.

\* \* \*

ALL THE MEN finished their beers, then left The Outlaw and mounted up. The bartender came to the door to watch, as if making sure they were really leaving so his customers would come back.

As they rode past the marshal's office, Ethan saw the man watching them from the window. He hoped he was right and the marshal wasn't Ashforth's informer in Kerrville.

Marshal Drover's "just south of town" turned out to be about two miles. The quarry was a large dug-out area which, as Drover said, could afford cover for a lot of men. It curved around so that they'd be able to hide their horses.

On the other hand, the men in the quarry could end up being trapped, if Ashforth had enough men to surround it.

"What d'ya think?" Granger asked.

"Could go either way," Ethan admitted.

"He might save us the trouble of findin' out, and not come," Granger said.

"I'm just worried he might. We'll get into a pitched battle with him and his men, and it'll turn out he didn't steal the weapons."

"Don't you think the army wants to get rid of him?" Granger asked.

"Yeah," Ethan said, "but they also want those weapons."

"Well," Granger said, "let's just figure on givin' them both."

# CHAPTER THIRTY-FOUR

T HEY RODE AS far as the rock quarry then reined in.
They sat on their horses and took a look at it.

"Some of us can take cover down in the quarry,"
Ethan said, "and others up above it, in those rocks.
That way we would avoid gettin' trapped."

Granger stood in his stirrups and looked all around.

"What is it?" Ethan asked.

Granger sat back down in his saddle.

"What if they don't come?" he asked.

"By the time we decide they're not comin'," Ethan
said "you and me, we'll come up with another idea."

"I'm glad you have so much faith in us, Ethan,"
Granger said.

"Actually," Ethan said, "it's you I have faith in,
Grange."

Sergeant Ezekial Jackson came over to join them.

"Should I send the men on ahead, Captain?" he asked.

"Yeah, Ezekial, do that," Ethan said. "We're gonna
hunker down here and wait."

"Yes, sir."

Jackson rode off to give the order.

"All right," Ethan said to Granger, "let's get 'em dismounted and placed, half down here, half up there."

"Horses around that bend, out of sight," Granger said.

"Right."

Granger nodded, turned his horse, and rode to where the rest of the men were gathered.

COLONEL ANTHONY ASHFORTH poured himself another glass of brandy and sat back in his rocking chair. He could hear his men being rowdy outside his house, which he'd had built just outside of Valverde. It was small, only two rooms, but it was perfect for him, since he lived in it alone. His men found their own lodging outside of the house, building a barracks, erecting tents. They could live there with as many men or women or children as they wanted. His only rule was that nobody went into the town of Valverde without his say-so.

Ashforth liked living alone. He had bunked with too many men during the war. Now he wanted his own space, and didn't want to share it with anyone else, man or woman. When he had a woman, she came and went, at his pleasure.

In fact, everything he did was for his pleasure, including the raids he and his men made. The war wasn't over for him, because, truth be told, he liked war. Riding for the Union, he hated the soldiers from both sides, and the people and way of life they were fighting over. But he loved the fighting and didn't want it to end. After the war he left the Union Army, promoted himself to colonel and came to South Texas. He quickly found men who felt the war shouldn't be over. Some felt as he did, some were still dedicated to the Confederacy, but it didn't matter to Ashforth why they rode with him, only that they did. The group became known as Ashforth's Raiders, a name which also suited him.

A knock on the door startled him from his reverie. He put his glass down. "Come!"

The door opened and Lieutenant Lionel Stanton entered. Stanton was his second-in-command.

"What is it, Stanton?"

"We just got word from Kerrville, Colonel," Stanton said.

"About what?"

"Negroes," Stanton said. "Twenty of them, ridin' with two white men."

"What were they doing in Kerrville?" Ashforth asked.

"They stopped in The Outlaw saloon and had beer," Stanton said, "then rode out."

"Do we know why they're in the area in the first place?" Ashforth asked.

"No, sir."

Ashforth thought a moment.

"They're probably a bunch of freed slaves looking to settle in the West," he said, finally.

"That's what I figured, sir," Stanton said.

"Well, we can't have that, can we?" Ashforth said. "Certainly not in our part of the West."

"No, sir."

"Assemble the men," Ashforth said.

"All of them, sir?"

"How any negroes are we talking about?"

"About twenty."

"How many men do we have, these days?"

"Forty-two," Stanton said. "That's including you and me."

"Then yes," Ashforth said. "Assemble them all."

"Yes, sir."

Stanton left the house and Ashforth rose. His coat

and hat of preference were a Confederate colonel's. He felt he looked better in gray than in blue. He put them on, then grabbed the saber he had taken from a real Confederate officer during the war. He strapped it on, then his gun, and stepped outside.

His rowdy men were now being gathered into a tight fighting force, strapping on their weapons, saddling their horses while Lieutenant Stanton shouted orders.

What were twenty niggers doing in South Texas, and why were they being led by two white men? That's what he intended to find out. And then make an example of them.

J ACKSON SENT HIS cousin Noah and another man, named Benson, on ahead to scout the area between the quarry and Valverde. As they approached the town they stopped.

"We was told not to go into town," Noah said. "Just look around."

"It looks like a quiet place," Benson said. "You think them raiders is in there?"

"No," Noah said, "they're probably not in town. But if they're here, they're around somewhere. Let's circle."

"Should we split up?"

"No," Noah said. "Ezekial said we was to stay together."

They changed direction, in order to go around Valverde.

I T WAS SOUTH of Valverde Noah and Benson found something.

"It looks like an old mining camp," Noah said. "But that house in the middle looks new."

The house sat by itself in amongst hastily erected

shacks and tents. While they watched, men swarmed out and began to saddle their horses.

"We better get outta here," Benson said.

He started to get to his feet, but Noah stopped him.

"Wait," he said, "look."

The front door of the small house opened and a man stepped out. He was dressed as a Confederate Colonel, complete with his saber.

"Oh Jesus," Benson said, "that be him?"

"Looks like it," Noah said. "Why else would he be here with so many men?"

"Look over there," Benson said, pointing.

Noah looked in the direction Benson was pointing, and saw the two wagons.

"Those are army wagons," Benson said, gripping Noah's arm with excitement. "I think we found the weapons."

"Take it easy," Noah said. "We don't wannabe seen or heard."

"So whatta we do?" Benson asked.

"You ride back to the quarry," Noah said, "tell 'em we found the camp, and the weapons. And tell them it look like Ashforth's Raiders are comin'."

"Whatta you gonna do?"

"If they all ride out, those wagons will be unprotected," Noah said.

"You can't take two of them," Benson said.

"I'll take one," Noah said. "When the captain gets here, he can take the other one."

"Noah, you're takin' a chance doin' this alone," Benson said.

"We can't let them weapons disappear again," Noah reasoned. "I'm jus' gonna see if I can hide 'em until the captain and the others get here."

"You ain't gon' do nothin' foolish, is you?" Benson asked.

"'Course I ain't," Noah said. "I ain't no foolish man. Now, you better ride. They'se gon' be mountin' up soon."

"Good luck," Benson said. "I'll see ya later."

Noah slapped the man on the back as he turned and ran to his horse.

While Noah watched he counted. There had to be more than forty, but less than fifty men. He wondered if Benson had noticed that and would pass it on? The only way the captain and the Buffalo Soldiers were going to defeat the superior numbers of raiders was by surprise. He hoped Captain Miller's plan would work.

A SHFORTH'S RAIDERS HAD a man named Dineen, who they used as a scout. He had experience fighting white men, Black men, and red men.

Stanton brought Dineen over to Colonel Ashforth, who was still standing on his porch.

"What is it?" Ashforth asked.

"Dineen's got somethin' to tell you, Colonel," Stanton said.

"Well? Out with it, man!"

"Yes, sir," Dineen, a small man in his thirties, said. "We're bein' watched, sir."

Ashforth had too much experience to react to that. He just kept his eyes straight.

"Where?"

"Above us, sir."

There was only one hill Dineen could have been talking about.

"All right," Ashforth said. "We're gonna ride out, Dineen. You take two men up that hill and see what you can find. Got it?"

"I got it, sir."

"If you find anybody, you bring them down here and wait till we get back."

"Yes, sir."

Ashforth looked at Stanton.

"The men ready?"

"Yessir."

"Then let's move 'em out," he said.

"Headed for where, sir?" Stanton said.

"Where else?" Ashforth said. "Valverde."

"Yes, sir!"


N OAH WATCHED AS the men finished mounting, and
then the colonel did the same. He raised his saber,
then brought it down in a slashing motion, and they
started moving. Noah immediately noticed that three
men veered away from the others. He turned and ran for
his horse.


D INEEN AND THE two other men got to the top of
the hill. The two remained mounted while Dineen
stepped down and examined the ground.

"So?" one of the men asked. "A ghost, or what?"

"There are footprints here," Dineen said. "Two men."
He pointed. "One went that way, the other that way."

"So one left," one of the men said. "Where's the
other one?"

Dineen looked down at their camp.

"I think I might know."


N OAH HASTILY MADE his way down off the hill, then
watched as the three men went up. He felt it would
take them a few minutes to read the situation. That
would give him enough time to check those wagons.

He rode into the camp, dismounted quickly, and hid
his horse behind the two Conestoga wagons. Hastily,

he climbed into one of them, saw the wooden crates. One of them had already been opened so he removed the top, and saw the army-issue rifles inside. They were Springfield 1866 breechloaders. He was sure the second wagon was going to be the same. He needed to get back to the Buffalo Soldiers and let Captain Miller know they had not only found Ashforth, but the weapons, as well.

He climbed out of the wagon, but when he turned to grab his horse's reins he found himself looking down the barrels of three guns.

# CHAPTER THIRTY-FIVE

W HEN BENSON REACHED the rock quarry he dismounted quickly and ran to Ethan.

"They're comin', Cap'n," he said, breathlessly.

"How many?" Ethan asked.

"They's gotta be forty or fifty," Benson guessed.

"Where's Noah?" Sergeant Jackson asked after his cousin.

"He wanted to stay and take a look at their camp," Benson said.

"What's it look like?" Ethan asked.

"Like an old mining camp," Benson said, "but not a rock quarry, like this one. They's a house in the middle of it. An officer came out, wearing Confederate Gray, and we figure it was Colonel Ashforth."

"Self-promoted colonel," Granger spat. "And the weapons?"

"They's two wagons there," Benson said. "Gotta have the weapons in 'em. Noah was gonna make sure."

"That fool," Jackson said. "He shouldn't have stayed there alone."

"All right," Ethan said, "let's get into position. Pass the word, Grange. Nobody starts shootin' until you and I do."

"Right."

Granger went to give the order.

A SHFORTH WAS LEADING his raiders toward Valverde when he realized something. He raised his hand to halt their progress.

"What is it, sir?" Lieutenant Stanton asked. Stanton was a young man who had been a sergeant during the war. He was happy to serve Ashforth and be promoted to lieutenant.

"I just realized between us and Kerrville there's an abandoned rock quarry. That would be a good place to spring an ambush. Twenty Black men in a saloon, that's somethin' they were sure would get around."

"You think they're trying to draw us in?" Stanton asked.

"I do," Ashforth said. "They've got two white men leadin' them. I wonder what that's about?"

"So what do we do?"

"Send a man on ahead. I want him to take a look at that rock quarry, but tell him to make sure nobody sees him."

"Yes, sir."

"The rest of us will remain here until he returns," Ashforth said.

Ashforth had it in mind to go back to their camp, but decided against it. First, he wanted to see what was going on at the quarry.

E THAN CALLED BENSON over.

"How far away do you think they were?" he asked.

"Not far behind me, sir," Benson said. "They shoulda been here by now."

"That's what I was thinkin'."

He sent the man back to his position, turned to talk to Granger and Jackson.

"Any sign of anyone?" Ethan asked. "He may have sent a scout up ahead."

"I haven't seen anyone," Jackson said.

"Me, neither," Granger said, "but . . ."

"But what?"

"I have the feelin' we're bein' watched," Granger said. "But it's just a feelin'."

"Well, more often than not your feelin's are right, Grange," Ethan said, without looking around. "If Ashforth sent a scout ahead, then we're all hidin' here for nothin'."

"I'm worried about my cousin Noah," Ezekial Jackson said.

"I think maybe we better go look for him," Ethan said.

"And what happens if we come face-to-face with Ashforth and his raiders?" Granger asked.

"I suppose we'll all start shootin'," Ethan said.

"What kind of a chance do we have that way?" Granger wondered.

"I guess we'll find out when the time comes," Ethan said. "Benson!"

Benson came running over.

"Yes, sir?"

"Can you find that camp?"

"Oh, yes, sir, I can."

"Then take the lead," Ethan said. "We're all gonna mount up and follow."

"Yes, sir."

Sergeant Jackson instructed all the Buffalo Soldiers to mount their horses and form a column of twos.

"The men are ready, sir," he told Ethan.

"Then let's get movin'," Ethan said, looking at the sky. "We don't want this confrontation takin' place at night."

They headed out, led by Benson.

A SHFORTH'S MAN RETURNED to where the raiders were waiting.

"You were right, sir," he said. "They would've been waitin' for us in the quarry."

"How many?"

"At least twenty."

"All Black except for two white men?"

"That's right."

Ashforth looked at Stanton.

"Tell the men we're going back."

"What are we gonna do when we get there, sir?" Stanton asked.

"We're going to wait."

I T'S JUST UP ahead, on the other side of that hill, sir," Benson said, pointing. "That's where I left Noah."

"Grange," Ethan said, and the two white men went up the hill. When they got near the top they got down on their bellies and crawled the rest of the way. They saw a man in a Confederate officer's uniform pacing back and forth in front of the house, his men milling about.

"That's Ashforth," Ethan said. "But where are his men? I don't see anythin' near forty or fifty. I see maybe . . . twelve."

"The rest are in hidin'," Granger said, "waitin' for us."

"Probably."

"You know," Granger said, "with a rifle I can kill him from here."

"Are you willin' to do that?" Ethan asked. "Kill a man from hidin'?"

"Well," Granger said, "in the war—"

"This isn't the war, Grange," Ethan said. "I'd like to bring the weapons and the men back to Fort Davis."

"Well, there're the wagons Benson mentioned," Granger said.

"But where's Noah?" Ethan asked.

"We can't let our concern for one man ruin our plans, Ethan," Granger said.

"I'm not sacrificin' anyone to this mission, Grange," Ethan Miller swore.

"So then how do you wanna play this, Ethan?" Granger asked him.

Ethan decided very quickly.

"I'll go down and talk to him," he said.

Granger looked shocked. "Alone?"

Ethan nodded.

"Don't forget the relationship the Colonel and me had durin' the war," Ethan said. "I'm hopin' I can play on that."

"He hated you," Granger said.

"If I remember correctly," Ethan said, "he hated everybody."

COLONEL ANTHONY ASHFORTH was surprised when he saw the lone man ride into his camp. And he was even more surprised when he recognized the man.

Lieutenant Stockton sidled up next to him.

"Do you know 'im?" he asked.

"I know him," Ashforth said. "Keep most of the men in the wagons and the house. We don't want to give away the strength and number of our force."

"Yes, sir."

Ashforth waited until the man reached him and reined in his horse.

"Captain Ethan Miller," he said.

"Should I be flattered you remember me, Lieutenant?" Ethan asked.

"It's Colonel, now."

"Of course it is."

"And you're still a captain?" Ashforth asked.

"No," Miller said. "I mustered out after the war. I'm a civilian contractor for the army."

"And in command of a company of freed slaves?" Ashforth asked.

"Not slaves, Ashforth," Ethan said. "Buffalo Soldiers."

Ashforth brightened.

"I did hear something about such a troop," he said. "But they were fighting Indians."

"This time," Ethan said, "they've been sent out to find you." He pointed. "And those weapons."

"Those weapons are now the property of the Army of the Confederacy."

"That army is dead, Ashforth," Ethan said. "You had a hand in killin' it, remember?"

"Not me," Ashforth said, "and not you. Robert E. Lee killed it."

"And you think you're the one who's gonna bring it back?" Ethan asked.

"That's exactly what I think," Ashforth said. "And you think you're gonna stop me?"

Ethan smiled grimly.

"That's exactly what I think, *Colonel* Ashforth," he said. "Exactly."

# CHAPTER THIRTY-SIX

"DISMOUNT, CAPTAIN," ASHFORTH said, "and we'll talk."

"I thought there was a chance you might shoot me from the saddle," Ethan admitted, dismounting. "Are we goin' inside?"

"We can talk right here, on the porch," Ashforth said. "I have two chairs."

"Whatever you like."

Ethan stepped onto the porch and the two men sat down, facing each other.

"I can't offer you any refreshments," Ashforth said. "Sorry."

Ethan looked at the door of the house. He had a good idea why they weren't going inside. He could see only two very small windows in the front wall, but he couldn't see inside.

"That's all right," Ethan said. "This really isn't a social call."

"No," Ashforth said, "you're here to attack me and take my weapons."

"The United States Army's weapons," Ethan said.

Ashforth smiled.

"Not anymore."

"You know," Ethan said, "I knew you were strange when we were servin' together, but I never thought you'd go this far."

"I was strange?" Ashforth said. "I was the one who wanted to fight the war. I mean, that's what a war is for, isn't it? To fight? You . . . you were more concerned about making friends, and having a pet nigger do for you."

"Easy, Lieutenant."

"That's *Colonel!*" Ashforth snapped. "Everybody here calls me Colonel."

Ethan looked out over the camp, saw the men who were still milling around, watching and waiting.

"All right, let's get to it, Colonel," Ethan said. "I need those guns. They need those guns at Fort Davis."

"And I need them here."

"You know I've got men surroundin' this camp."

"I've got men, Captain," Ashforth said, "you've got niggers."

"You're right, I do," Ethan said, "and a lot of them are still mad about the war, and what went on before it. They're dyin' for me to give a signal for them to come down here."

"Tell them to come on down," Ashforth said. "I outnumber you two to one."

"You would out in the open," Ethan said, "but right now most of your men are either in those wagons, or in this house. They're not doin' you much good there."

Ashforth frowned.

"See, you thought you were smart, hidin' your men, but what you did was put them where they can't do you any good, in a little house with small windows."

Ashforth looked at the door.

"And another thing," Ethan said. "You should've killed me as soon as you saw me, but you wanted to gloat. And I figured on that."

Ashforth looked up toward the hill.

"No, my men aren't up there," Ethan said. "They're down here already."

Ashforth looked over at the two wagons, where Black men were now pulling white men out, under the barrels of their guns.

"And you smell that?" Ethan asked. "Somethin's burnin'. What d'ya think it is?"

Ashforth sniffed the air, then heard somebody from inside the house shout, "Help, we're on fire!"

Ethan knew that two of the Buffalo Soldiers had snuck down behind the hose with torches and lit the back wall. Other soldiers, under the command of Sergeant Jackson, had surprised the raiders who were hiding in the weapons wagons.

All Ashforth had were the dozen or so men he had left out in front of the house, as some pitiful show of force.

Ashforth stood up quickly.

"Easy," Ethan said, pointing his pistol.

The twelve men stared up at the colonel, waiting for orders. Meanwhile, still more Buffalo Soldiers came from around the back of the house, with their rifles already raised.

The front door of the house opened, but as a man tried to leave, Ethan shot him. He fell back into the arms of another man, who now had second thoughts about coming through the door.

The twelve men in front dropped their guns and

raised their hands. The men who had climbed out of the wagons also had their hands up. They numbered about two dozen. That meant there were at least sixteen men in the now burning building. Ethan waved two of the Buffalo Soldiers over.

"Keep your guns trained on that door," he said. "Anybody tries to come out with a gun, kill 'em."

"Yes, sir," the two men said.

"Drop your gun, Ashforth."

Ashforth undid his gun belt and let it drop.

"Now let's get off this porch," Ethan said. "We don't wanna burn, do we?"

"Are you going to let those men burn inside?" Ashforth asked.

"Why not?" Ethan asked. "You were going to have them kill me and my men."

"I didn't think you had this in you," Ashforth admitted.

"You were always bad at strategy, Tony," Ethan said. "That's why I never took your advice."

The men inside the house were now yelling and screaming.

"Tell 'em they can come out without their guns," Ethan told Ashforth.

"You men in the house!" Ashforth shouted. "Come out with your hands empty and you won't be shot."

Ethan waited. One man appeared, his hands empty, and hesitantly stepped outside, coughing. Then another, and a third. Soon all the men—except the one Ethan had shot—were standing outside, coughing and blinking their eyes while smoke billowed from the small house.

Granger came walking over. Behind him was Sergeant Ezekial Jackson and Gabriel, supporting their cousin, Noah, between them.

"Is he all right?" Ethan asked.

"Yes, sir," Jackson said. "He got much worse beatings back on the plantation."

"What are we gonna do with all these men?" Granger asked.

"Well, first toss their guns in those wagons with the other weapons. Then hitch up two teams."

"Are we takin' them all back to Fort Davis?" Granger asked.

"No," Ethan said, "we're takin' the weapons, and Colonel Ashforth, here. The rest of them can stay where they are."

"They'll just start raidin' again," Granger said.

"Not without a leader," Ethan said. "Not without weapons, or horses."

"Horses?" Granger said.

"Oh, I forgot to tell you," Ethan said. "Scatter all their horses."

Ashforth was staring at Ethan with hatred in his eyes. He was still trying to accept the fact that Ethan had outmaneuvered him and captured all of his men, all the while firing one single shot.

Sergeant Jackson tied Ashforth's hands behind him, and then relieved him of his saber. The raiders had all been gathered in the center of the compound, where they were sitting on the ground. Some of them were still coughing and rubbing their teary eyes.

Granger came over to Ethan.

"I gotta admit, I didn't think this would work," Granger said.

"The only way it wouldn't have worked was if he had shot me on sight," Ethan said, "which was what he should've done. But he hated me and had to gloat."

"Which you counted on."

"That's right."

"It's a good thing you knew him so well," Granger said.

* * *

THE BUFFALO SOLDIERS got the army wagons hitched up and ready to go. They got Ashforth up on his horse, his hands still tied behind him. All of his men sat on the ground and watched helplessly.

Ethan walked over to them.

"Who was second-in-command, here?" he asked.

"That'd be me," one man said. "Lieutenant Stanton."

"You fight in the war, Stanton?"

"Yes, sir."

"What was your rank there."

"Sergeant."

"For the Confederacy?"

"Yes, sir."

"Do you know that the war is over, Sergeant?"

"Yes, sir."

"Do any of you men think the Civil War ain't over?"

Nobody answered.

"When we leave here, my advice to all of you is that you start walkin' home," Ethan said. "Go home and start your lives again. Count yourselves lucky that you came out of this little skirmish alive and well. Your colonel, who was only a lieutenant in the war, will be going to the guardhouse for a long stay. Forget him. Start over."

"Captain," Stanton said, "we'll die out here."

"We took your guns and your horses," Ethan said. "We're leavin' you water. Kerrville is not so far that you can't walk it. But the law there will be waitin' for you, so make sure you don't try to start any trouble there."

"Mister," another man said, "I'm just goin' home."

"I'm goin' the other way," another man said, "to Mexico. It's closer."

"It's probably a good idea for all of you to split up," Ethan said.

He turned and walked to where Granger was holding his horse for him. He mounted up, looked back at the men who were seated on the ground, then raised his hand and yelled out, "Forward!"

The weapons wagons, driven by Buffalo Soldiers, started moving, along with the mounted men. Ethan and Granger kept Ashforth between them.

"You really think it's smart to leave them?" Granger asked.

"It's that," Ethan said, "or execute them all. You wanna do that, Grange?"

# CHAPTER THIRTY-SEVEN

T HE AVERY FAMILY was pleasantly surprised when the Buffalo Soldiers pulled into their camp with their two wagons, and all their men.

"We didn't expect you back so soon," William Avery said to Ethan.

"To tell you the truth, William," Ethan said, "we didn't know if we'd get back, at all."

Ethan and the Buffalo Soldiers had spent one night camped after they recovered the weapons and captured Ashforth. They kept an all-night vigil, in case Ashforth's men reassembled. But it didn't happen. Ethan was pretty certain that Ashforth's Raiders had been completely demoralized by the events.

Ashforth himself maintained a sullen silence all the way back to Kerrville.

Marshal Ed Drover was also surprised when Ethan walked into his office, leading a trussed-up Ashforth.

"I'm guessin' things went well for you," he said.

"We got lucky," Ethan said. "I'd like to put him in a cell for the night. We'll be out of your hair tomorrow."

"Suits me," Drover said.

He took Ashforth into the cell block and locked him in, then returned to the office, where Ethan waited.

"I'll supply some men to keep an eye on him while he's here," Ethan said.

"I've got a part-time deputy who can sit here with him," Drover said.

"That's okay," Ethan said. "I've got enough men that they can switch off every couple of hours."

"Suit yourself," Drover said. "I'd like to meet up with you over at The Outlaw, though, buy you a beer and hear the story."

"That's fine," Ethan said. "And I'll have my men go into the saloon a few at a time, so as not to drive customers out."

"That'll be appreciated."

The door opened and two Black men entered, armed with rifles.

"These are two of my men," Ethan said. "They'll sit with Ashforth the first two hours."

"Then we might as well go and have that beer," Drover said.

"Lead the way," Ethan said.

WHEN ETHAN RETURNED to the Avery camp Alice Avery handed him a cup of coffee.

"Supper will be in a couple of hours," she told him. "We're so happy to have you back here."

"We're happy to be back, ma'am."

He heard children laughing and then saw that they were chasing Gabriel around the camp.

"The children love him," Alice said.

"Are they fully recovered from the Apache attack?" Ethan asked.

"There's still a bad dream or two," Alice admitted. "But for the most part they're fine," she told him. "Having you all here will help."

"We'll be headin' out in the mornin', ma'am. We can get your family as far as Fort Davis, and then you can decide what you want to do."

"We appreciate that, Captain."

Ethan walked over to where Granger was standing by the recovered weapons wagons.

"Looks like they're all there, Ethan," he said. "The cartons were pried open, but apparently they ain't done anythin' with these weapons, yet."

"What've we got?" Ethan asked.

"Springfield sixty-sixes. Enough to outfit a couple of forts."

"Colonel Merritt's gonna be very happy with this outcome." Ethan said.

"And we'll get paid," Granger said. "Finally."

"We'd better," Ethan said. "I'm ready to return to Paradise."


THE NEXT MORNING the Avery family got their wagons packed, Ethan picked up Ashforth from the marshal's office, and they got the four wagons, the Avery family, and the Buffalo Soldiers headed for Fort Davis.

Ethan was hoping they presented enough of a show of force to keep Comanches or Apaches from trying to raid them on the trail.

The trip back was a lot more leisurely, especially without any sort of enforced forty-five-day deadline. As it turned out they didn't encounter any trouble with Indians, didn't suffer any injuries or damaged weapons, and pulled up to the gate of Fort Davis with everything they had been sent out to get, and more.

* * *

COLONEL MERRITT CAME out of his office as the wagons pulled to a stop. Ethan dismounted and dragged Ashforth down from his horse.

"Colonel Merritt, meet former Lieutenant Anthony Ashforth, who has been callin' himself Colonel. And there," he turned and pointed, "are your weapons."

"By God," Merritt said, "you did it, man!" He turned to his adjutant. "Lieutenant Foley, have this man taken to the guardhouse."

"Yes, sir."

A couple of soldiers took charge of Ashforth. Ethan was happy to have the man off his hands.

"Captain Miller," Merritt said, "why don't you come inside and give me your report?"

"My pleasure, sir."

"Lieutenant," Merritt said to Lieutenant Foley, "Have these Buffalo Soldiers taken to their new barracks. They've earned it."

Ethan followed Merritt into his office, beckoning to Granger to join them.

MERRITT LISTENED TO Ethan's oral report of everything that had happened since he and the Buffalo Soldiers left Fort Davis. He then informed Ethan that the horses he had delivered had all been broken.

"Here," he said, taking an envelope out of his desk, "is your payment in full. I believe you'll find it's the correct amount."

Ethan looked at the letter of payment, which he would be able to present to his bank in Montana.

"We don't have that much cash on hand," Merritt said. "I hope your men will be able to wait till they're home to get paid."

"They'll just have to put off a visit to El Paso for another time," Ethan said.

"They can celebrate in Bozeman," Granger said, "or Helena, when we get back."

"When will you be leaving?" Merritt asked.

"Tomorrow morning," Ethan said. "There's just one more thing."

"What's that?"

"The Avery family has been through a lot," Ethan explained. "But I believe they're still intent on making it all the way to California."

"I'll have them safely escorted out of Texas," Merritt said. "And I might be able to have them seen safely through Arizona."

"That'd be great," Ethan said. He looked at Granger. "Anythin' else?"

"Not for me," Granger said.

"Then I guess our business is done," Ethan said to Merritt.

"Unless you'd like to re-up?" Merritt asked. "I think we might even be able to get you a promotion to major."

"Colonel," Ethan said, standing, "that's not somethin' I'm even the least bit tempted to do." He shook the man's hand rather than salute.

"The US Army thanks you, Mr. Miller," Merritt said.

Ethan and Granger left the colonel's office.

"You wanna break the news to the men that they're not gettin' paid till we get home? Or should I?" Granger asked, out front.

"They're my men," Ethan said. "I'll tell 'em. After bein' stuck here breakin' broncs all this time, I'm thinkin' they might be lookin' forward to goin' home."

"They were lookin' forward to goin' to El Paso and bustin' loose," Granger said.

"Well, let's look at it this way," Ethan said. "We won't end up havin' to bail anyone out of jail."

Ready to find
your next great read?

Let us help.

**Visit prh.com/nextread**